AULETRIS

EROTICA

by

ANAÏS NIN

Anaïs Nin in Provincetown, 1941. Photo: José Alemany

SKY BLUE PRESS
San Antonio, Texas

Library of Congress Cataloging-in-Publication Data

Names: Nin, Anaïs, 1903-1977, author. Herron, Paul (Paul S.),
editor, writer of introduction.
Nin, Anaïs, 1903-1977. Marcel. | Nin, Anaïs,
1903-1977. Life in Provincetown.
Title: Auletris : erotica / by Anaïs Nin ; edited by Paul Herron ;
introduction by Paul Herron.
Description: San Antonio, Texas : Sky Blue Press, [2016]
Identifiers: LCCN 2016029894 | ISBN 9780988917095
(softcover : acid-free paper)
Subjects: | GSAFD: Erotic fiction.
Classification: LCC PS3527.I865 A6 2016 | DDC 813/.54--dc23
LC record available at https://lccn.loc.gov/2016029894

This book is dedicated to the memory of John Ferrone.

ACKNOWLEDGMENTS

"Marcel" from DELTA OF VENUS Erotica by Anaïs Nin. Copyright © 1969 by Anaïs Nin. Copyright © 1977 by The Anaïs Nin Trust. Used by permission of Houghton Mifflin Harcourt Publishing Company. All rights reserved.

Special thanks to the Special Collections Department of the Charles E. Young library at UCLA for providing a copy of *Auletris* for this publication.

Thanks to Benjamin Franklin V, whose advice concerning the Introduction was extremely helpful.

Cover art: from the personal collection of Anaïs Nin.

INTRODUCTION

Aaïs Nin is considered by many as the godmother or, as Nin herself put it, the Madame[1] of feminine erotica, and in writing for a collector at a dollar a page she risked arrest, conviction and imprisonment because of the draconian obscenity laws of the 1940s. In spite of the danger and the much-needed income, Nin didn't take her erotic writing seriously—she said that she "was writing to entertain, under pressure from a client" and that she believed her "style was derived from men's work"[2]—but when it was finally published as *Delta of Venus* and *Little Birds* in the 1970s, it became her bestselling work and gave her name a notoriety that has survived for a generation.

After the publication of Nin's erotica, Harcourt editor John Ferrone declared that only unpublishable scraps of the original remained.[3] So how, then, is it possible that a major work of Nin erotica included in this volume has remained unknown to the public and Nin insiders alike for decades?

Auletris was originally typed on latrine rag (onion paper) with four carbons, making a total of five copies, which were bound into books by the Press of the Sunken Eye (Carmel) in 1950. It consists of two stories. One of them is the unedited version of "Marcel" that appears in an abbreviated form in *Delta of Venus*, and the other is "Life in Provincetown," which was unknown to Nin's literary executor, editor and literary agent, all of whom had a deep and vast knowledge of her work. There is no such manuscript in Nin's archives. Here is how, based on the facts we now have, I believe *Auletris* came to be.

It is widely known that Nin began writing erotica in the early 1940s for a collector or "patron" whose agent was a man named Barnett Ruder in New York. According to Nin's diary, Henry Miller met Ruder in 1940 and was offered a job that would pay him "one hundred dollars a month to write one hundred pages or so especially for [Ruder]—mostly on sex."[4] Miller was in serious need of money, so he accepted. He began writing with the understanding that Ruder was sending his work to a collector who financed the operation, although Miller suspected that Ruder himself was the actual collector.[5] The writing soon became drudgery, and Miller felt enslaved. When Doubleday offered him a contract for a "book on America," which eventually became *The Air-Conditioned Nightmare*, Miller dropped the erotic writing altogether.

Nin, who was Miller's longtime lover and *patronne*, agreed to finance Miller's tour of America for the new book. To raise funds, she suggested showing Ruder a revised version of her 1932 diary, which contained the sexually charged passages about the beginning of Nin's relationship with Miller and his wife June.[6] She also "pasted one of [her] most becoming Louveciennes photographs on the cover."[7] The package was given to Ruder, who said he would see if his patron, an "old millionaire down south," approved. Not surprisingly, he did, and Nin's career of literary prostitution, as she called it, began.

Between 1940 and 1942 Nin produced at least 850 pages of erotica, not including what was written by a group of literary friends she gathered together to increase the page count. Nin, who rarely destroyed any of her writing, kept the carbons for more than thirty years. In the 1970s her Los Angeles lover Rupert Pole felt there was a bestseller wasting away in her archive.[8] Nin, who discounted the erotic writing as imitative of male porno-graphers, nixed the idea of publishing it, fearing it would damage her standing in literature. But Pole was persistent, and after a long period of cajoling, he persuaded her to let John Ferrone offer a professional opinion.[9]

It was nearly a year later that Ferrone read the story "The Hungarian Adventurer" on a visit to Pole and Nin in Los Angeles. He was convinced that Pole was right about the erotica and that Nin was wrong. Ferrone told Nin that her erotica was not imitative of male writing at all, but uniquely feminine, rich, beautifully written, literary and ground-breaking. Nin agreed to let Harcourt publish the erotica and told Ferrone he could edit it however he thought best.[10] Ferrone took the entire collection with him back to New York and set about the massive task of unraveling the complicated and entangled tales and make them into cohesive stories. Because Nin was seriously ill with cancer by then, Ferrone wasn't able to ask for her opinions or explanations and was completely on his own.

The initial collection, *Delta of Venus*, was published only months after Nin's death in 1977. It became an instant critical and commercial success, remaining on *The New York Times* best-seller list for thirty-six weeks, and, as Ferrone later noted, "[m]ore royalties would pour in from the sales of *Delta* than from all of [Nin's] previous books put together."[11] *The New York Times Book Review* called *Delta of Venus* "a joyous display of the erotic imagination," and *Cosmopolitan* said it was "inventive, sophisticated" and "highly elegant naughtiness." *Little Birds*, the second volume of Nin erotica, also edited by Ferrone, enjoyed similar success two years later.

Ferrone said that "[s]lightly more than half of the 850 pages ended up in *Delta*, and another thirty percent was used in the second volume, *Little Birds.* The rest, about a hundred pages of fragments and trimmings, was left unpublished."[12] Ferrone had no reason to believe that there was any viable Nin erotica yet to be published. Then, in 1985, he received a letter from a colleague telling him that Harris Auction Galleries in Baltimore had approached Harcourt seeking bibliographic information on Anaïs Nin, which was nothing unusual. But the letter contained a bombshell: Harris claimed it was about to auction off a book called *Auletris* that consisted of two erotic stories written by "A. Nin," and that one of them "might be a discovery."[13] While one of the stories ("Marcel") was familiar to the Harcourt editors, the other, "Life in Provincetown," was unknown to all concerned. Could it be that somehow a major piece of Nin erotica had been lost for four decades and was suddenly found?

The volume of *Auletris* Harris was planning to auction off was copy no. 3 of 5. While there is no definitive proof that any copies were sold, a penciled-in price of $35.00 for copy no. 3 indicates it is possible. Copy no. 1 is housed at UCLA, no. 2 is in the collection of the late Alvaro Cardona-Hine and no. 4 is found in the George Howard Papers at USC. The locations of nos. 3 and 5 are unknown.

George Howard was based in Los Angeles in the early 1940s and was befriended by Miller. Miller suggested that Nin send typescripts of the erotica written for Ruder to Howard for possible sale in California.[14] According to the contents list of his archive, Howard had copies of not only the stories in *Auletris*, but much of the erotica included in *Delta of Venus* and *Little Birds*, as well as the stories in Miller's *Opus Pistorum*. According to Miller biographer Robert Ferguson, Howard had offered the stories of *Opus* to a friend of Miller's[15] in 1950. When the friend asked Miller about the stories, Miller denied writing them[16], though many Miller scholars believe he is indeed the author.

The Miller stories were ostensibly collected in *Opus Pistorum* by Press of the Sunken Eye in 1950, the same year that Howard had tried to sell them to Miller's friend. Press of the Sunken Eye issued *Auletris* during the same year. Since both Miller and Nin had sent Howard copies of their erotica, and we know that Howard was trying to sell Miller's, it is probable that he also tried to sell Nin's and eventually found a buyer for both.

According to Harris Galleries' description of *Auletris*, the man who retyped *Auletris* and *Opus Pistorum* was Milton Luboviski[17]. Both books were produced by Press of the Sunken Eye in 1950, and while they were created with different typewriters, Harris Galleries says that "the format of both works is very similar."[18] Both books were typed with four carbons, adding up to five copies each, including the ribbon copy.

So we have an idea of how "Life in Provincetown" and "Marcel" wound up in Luboviski's hands,
but why was "Life in Provincetown" unknown for so
long? Was it that the story somehow got lost during
the three decades the carbons were in Nin's
archive? This seems unlikely because Nin was
organized and meticulous when it came to her
work—the only major item that she ever lost was a
volume of her childhood diary.[19] Perhaps the
typescript she sent to Miller was the only one. It
could be that she didn't notice this, or perhaps she
sent it to Howard with the understanding he would
send it back after copying it. There is also a January
10, 1942 letter[20] from Miller to Howard asking
about a "missing folder of erotica." Could "Life in
Provincetown" have been in that folder?

Since there seems to be no original carbon of
"Life in Provincetown" in existence, how can we be
certain it is Nin's work? And if it is her work, how
do we know that Luboviski or someone else didn't
tinker with it?

Nin's prose style is distinct, with unique
terminology and phrasing. In other words, her work
is easily recognized. "Life in Provincetown" fits in
seamlessly with the stories in *Delta of Venus* and
Little Birds, and there is nothing that would make a
seasoned Nin reader suspicious of its authorship.
Furthermore, it appears with an erotic story known
to be by her, "Marcel." It is unlikely that anyone

would use a Nin story with a non-Nin story in the same book. As for Luboviski editing the story, we must consider that he was merely trying to make money off someone else's work. What incentive would there have been to edit or rewrite passages? One indication of editing would have been textual or stylistic alterations to "Marcel," but when compared to the *Delta* version, the only significant changes are extensive cuts by Ferrone. For this reason, it is logical to conclude that "Life in Provincetown" appears as Nin wrote it.

It is obvious that whoever wrote "Life in Provincetown" was familiar with the town and the artists' community within. We know from Nin's diaries that she spent a good deal of time in Provincetown in the 1940s, and she was sexually involved with some people she met there.[21]

The *Auletris* version of "Marcel" is 51 pages long, as opposed to the 17 pages in *Delta of Venus*. John Ferrone said that there were two major reasons for heavy edits in the erotica—one was that "many [stories] had to be carved out of long, episodic narratives that contained tales within tales. They needed beginnings and endings, and often titles as well."[22] The other was censorship. Ferrone says that "[i]t was clear from the beginning that Anaïs, never dreaming of publication, had drawn on the outlines of her own life for inspiration, as well as on the Kama Sutra and

Krafft-Ebing. It would have been easy for readers to mistake fiction for autobiography. There were many other autobiographical parallels, some probably close to fact. It becomes evident [...] that Anaïs borrowed heavily from her journal material, as she did for all of her fiction."[23] Because some of the characters were based on people still living, Ferrone felt the need to either render them unrecognizable or to excise them altogether. Today, no such restrictions exist.

Why didn't Harcourt, or anyone else, publish *Auletris*? It's easy to see why no one in 1986 would republish any version of "Marcel," the heavily edited version of which was already included in *Delta of Venus*. And perhaps because of the odd length of "Life in Province-town" (43 typewritten pages), it wouldn't make sense for a commercial publisher to release it on its own.

This edition of *Auletris* is reproduced as it appears in the original, minus misspellings, typos and minor formatting problems, allowing the reader to see Nin's words as they were intended for the collector, as well as providing an opportunity to see how John Ferrone went about creating a bestseller from the raw material.

—*Paul Herron, August 2016*

Works Cited

Dearborn, Mary. *The Happiest Man Alive: A Biography of Henry Miller*. New York: Simon & Schuster, 1991.

Ferguson, Robert. *Henry Miller: A Life*. New York: W. W. Norton, 1991.

Ferrone, John. "The Making of *Delta of Venus*," *A Café in Space: The Anaïs Nin Literary Journal*, volume 7. Santa Fe, NM: Sky Blue Press, 2010.

Nin, Anaïs. *The Diary of Anaïs Nin 1939-1943* (volume 3). New York: Harcourt Brace Jovanovich, 1969.

----. *Linotte: The Early Diary of Anaïs Nin, 1914-1920*. New York: Harcourt Brace Jovanovich, 1978.

----. *Mirages: The Unexpurgated Diary of Anaïs Nin, 1939-1947*. Athens, OH: Swallow Press/Sky Blue Press, 2013.

Notes

[1] On November 4, 1941, Nin writes: "I gather the poets around me, and persuade them to write erotica, communicating eroticism and spreading this writing that is usually suppressed, giving them both the poison of disintegration and perhaps a way of purification, for all of us have violent explosions of poetry, and we eject the purely sexual as fervently as if we had taken vows of chastity. A purge, and not debauchery, results from the infiltration of erotic confessions. [Harvey] Breit, [George] Barker, Robert [Duncan]. A house of prostitution. I, the Madame, supplying the Old Man with moments of perverse felicity, his drug..." (*Mirages*, p. 81)

[2] Postscript to the Introduction of *Delta of Venus*, p. xvi.

[3] Ferrone, p. 56.

[4] *Mirages*, p. 42.

[5] *Diary 3*, pp. 56-57.

[6] *Mirages*, p. 41. Nin writes: "I could give [Ruder] copies of the diary in exchange for money for Henry's trip. Virginia [Admiral] copied diary 32, I revised it, changed the names…"

[7] *Mirages*, p. 42.

[8] Ferrone, p. 53.

[9] Ferrone, p. 54.

[10] Ferrone, p. 55.

[11] Ferrone, p. 59.

[12] Ferrone, p. 56.

[13] In a letter to Rupert Pole dated January 16, 1986, Ferrone says that Harris Galleries had "two of Anaïs's erotica manuscripts, bound. One is called 'Marcel,' and was published in *Delta*. The other is called 'Life in Provincetown' and appears to not have been published."

[14] In Box 1, Folder 2 of the Howard archive, a letter dated March 26, 1941 and signed by Anaïs Nin asks Howard if he wishes to see more pages of the manuscripts from which Miller had previously given him a sample. She also entreats him to suggest a way of disposing of the manuscript in order to finance Miller's tour of America.

In Box 1, Folder 3, there is a letter dated October 11, 1941 and signed by Henry Miller in which he says that he is sending Howard a typescript of pornographic material done by Nin and informing Howard of an abridged version of the Diary, which covers 1930-1935 in Paris.

[15] Ferguson cites a letter from Miller's friend Rives Childs in which he tells Miller the names of the stories Howard offered him. Miller flatly denied writing the stories. (*Henry Miller: A Life*, pp. 277-278.)

[16] Ferguson posits that Miller may have been "ashamed" of his role in pornography (p. 277). Another Miller biographer, Mary Dearborn, thinks that Miller was continuing to "distance himself from Nin in deference to her wishes that their relationship remain secret" (p. 211). Neither biographer questions Miller's authorship of *Opus Pistorum*.

[17] Milton Luboviski, in his "Epilogue" of the 1983 Grove Press edition of *Opus Pistorum*, claimed that Miller wrote for him in the early 1940s, which counters Ferguson's (and Nin's) account that he wrote the original material for Ruder.

[18] From a rough draft of the description of *Auletris*, Harris Galleries, 1986.

[19] "A manuscript of the diary covering the period from January 1918 to March 1919 was lost." *Linotte*, p. 207.

[20] The letter is in Box 1, Folder 7 of the George Howard papers.

[21] See pp. 58-85 in *Mirages*.

[22] The *Auletris* version of "Marcel" contains fragments of other stories that appear in *Delta of Venus*, including "Mathilde," "Mandra" and "Miriam."

[23] Ferrone, p. 56.

AULETRIS

by

"A. Nin"

"The tongue is woman's weapon."—Canterbury

BOOK ONE

LIFE IN PROVINCETOWN

One long main street running along the Bay outline, Portuguese fishermen sitting in circles like the Italians and chatting. Behind the houses on the main street are wharves which project out on the water at various lengths. On these wharves are the huts, shacks, which the fishermen once used to store their nets, tools, and the boats to be repaired. It is here that the artists live. The roofs are peaked and beamed. Everything is made of rough wood like the inside of some old ship. At high tide the water runs under the wharves, at low tide it exposes a long stretch of sand.

The walls are thin. One can hear everything. Often the shades are not down, and one can see everything.

There are no guardians, no one to say: stop the noise, or to see at what time one comes home. No superintendents, house owners. Just the lonely wharves, in darkness at night, the sound of the water, and little crooked shack-like studios occupied by a variety of people.

The town is full of soldiers, sailors, and beautiful Portuguese girls...and summer visitors in shorts.

There is one movie, one bar where women are not admitted and several night clubs.

In one studio there lived one of the artist's models, whose mouth was so big, so full, so prominent, that one could see nothing else. When she looked at one, one could notice only the mouth, like the mouth of a negress. She rouged too heavily, and then powdered her face white, so that the mouth stood out even more and was able to eclipse the rest of the face and even the body.

As one knew she was a model, well known in the Village in New York, one assumed she had a beautiful body, but somehow one only looked at the mouth. Somehow or other one imagined the other mouth to be equally luxuriant, equally prominent. Just as one felt that the thin-lipped mouths of Puritan women must he the exact replicas of their thin-lipped sexuality.

This mouth wore a flaming red bathing suit from morning till evening. She lived alone with the shades always up. One could watch her dress in the morning. One could see her asleep, first of all, late in the morning, sprawled on her bed in great disorder. That was when she was alone. She was rarely alone. Very often she lay in bed completely concealed by some heavy arm, or a man's body...

They slept as if they had had a bout and were exhausted. Slept on through the morning, in each other's arms. Locked as they were, it was difficult to imagine that this locked embrace was only temporary. The next evening it would be a different man. The model had such a simple way of solving her problem. When she saw a handsome man in the street, she slipped her arm through his, looked up at his face, smiling, and said, "Hello."

It was as simple as that. Rarely was she given a cold hello because of her mouth.

Unlocking herself from the embrace of her night visitor she would rush to her work as a model, so everyone in Provincetown knew her body more or less intimately. The painting classes knew it from long hours of contemplation, and the rest of the town, from such bouts as I have mentioned.

The only one she could not lure so easily to her room was her very own neighbor, the handsomest boy in all the town, the son of a Portuguese fisherman, now captain of a sailing yacht which took visitors around the Cape at night for one dollar.

He slept next door to her. Before he had seen her he had heard all the tumult in her room; the night before, he had heard a particular grunt of satisfaction from some heavy body, and then a woman's delighted laughter, such a laughter as he had never heard.

To begin with he had never heard of a woman laughing while love-making. They always grew so serious and intense, the gayest of them. He had known plenty in his sailor life. They always grew serious. Never even smiled, as if love-making, even with a stranger, were an intense affair, not to be treated lightly.

Their pleasure was always like the pleasure of an animal, dark rather, with strange sounds.

Animals do not laugh. Women became animals at night, surely, as these legends told us. More so even than men.

But not the richly-mouthed model. She laughed like a negress being tickled. Every caress made her laugh obscenely. And there was a different kind of laughter for each part of the body. Lying in the dark, on the other side of the wall, he could almost divine where she was being touched.

At first it was her feet, surely, and it tickled her because she giggled. It must have been only the external portions of her body, for she laughed gaily, lightly. The man with her must have been touching her ribs, her shoulders, her arms, her legs. Suddenly, her laughter changed. It was modulated as if she were being slightly hurt, and it was that she was growing vulnerable.

He could tell. She laughed like someone plunging into too cold water, and gasping, and then feeling the warm reaction, and enjoying the new sensation.

She laughed as if pleasure were new and beginning to invade her. Ah.....ahh.....came her voice in the darkness. If he could have seen her move he would not have been as clearly aware of her pleasure. He felt this pleasure of hers rippling through his muscles. The walls were so thin he could feel it all in his body. Ah.....ahh.....there was a silence. This silence disturbed the Portuguese more than anything. What could keep her so still, after her rippling and open pleasure? What caress could silence her suddenly as if too profound to cause an exterior proof of joy? He tried to divine. He knew she was naked, for he had heard her say, "Let's take all our clothes off." What was the man doing to her? No sound. The Portuguese felt ripples covering his strong, dark body. He felt close to a mystery. He expected her to cry out any moment from uncontainable ecstasy. Instead there came out of the darkness, a long, prolonged low laughter, guttural, rich, low, obscene...

The other mouth—surely the man had opened his way into the other mouth, the luxuriant, thick, rich sexual mouth she carried almost exposed for everyone to see in her twin mouth of her face...for everyone to see the thickness and fullness of her sexual feelings...ripe and open and red... Ah..... Ah.....came the voice. The flesh indented by the attack of the man, yielding, and with guttural cries that revealed the thrusts made into it, each thrust accompanied by a long ahhhhhh.....ahhhhhhh of pleasure, until her voice sank.

And then again a silence. And then the voice came as if she were suddenly violently wounded. Ahhh........ The Portuguese's body was burning, tortured with desire. Each cry of the woman raised his penis in the dark. And how it burned. All the wind and sun that had beaten against it, the cold and heat, the salt water, contributed to making it firm and salty and vigorous, and now it stood raised in the dark, leaping at each modulation of the woman's voice. When her last cry came, he almost thought he would come too, so feverish and taut he was, listening to this scene and imagining all its developments...

Silence now. They must have fallen asleep. The Portuguese could not sleep. He rose and slipped on his trousers. He opened the screen door of his studio. There was a light next door. The shades were raised. And there she lay, naked and asleep, with the man fallen over her. No matter how much he desired her, and now it was every moment of the day and night, when he saw her walking about, so naked in her bathing suit that he could see the curled pubic hairs protruding on each side of her tight panties, so naked that the straps often fell from her shoulders and revealed half of her breasts...yet he could not bring himself to become one of those anonymous men who could all give her pleasure.

He could not bring himself to take this body which belonged to everyone and could enjoy any-one's caresses equally. That held him back.

And what difficulty he had in being reserved with her and yet having to listen almost every night to the same scene.

She was indefatigablc... "She's a nymphomani-ac," he thought. "She never has enough...she is a monster... I don't want to love a monster like that. She is just like her mouth, big and voracious and always hungry. I could never keep her to myself..."

That is not what she thought. She felt somehow, that right next door to her lived the most vigorous of them all. She sensed his vigor. She could not break down his resistance. And then with a feminine clairvoyance she divined what kept him away from her. She decided to sacrifice to him the days of her pleasure. She felt sure or her plan.

Suddenly no one came to see her. Every night he listened and there was no sound of love-making. She lay in her bed, and he could hear her turning over. He could hear the hair pins dropping on the floor when she loosened her hair. But no love-making. He was intrigued. He began to think more and more about her.

One night he heard her sigh. He was unable to sleep. He raised his voice a little and said: "Why are you sighing?"

"I'm here alone and I am remembering a terrible story l heard today. I met a woman on the beach who talked to me. She was a curious, handsome woman, highly strung. Her hands trembled all the time. We started talking. She described her son to me. When he was thirteen he was a beautiful boy with long eyelashes like a girl, a slender body, a fine crop of curly brown hair. He was clever and brilliant.

"They lived in Paris. The boy was abnormally fond of reading. Especially the poets. At thirteen he had already tried smoking and drinking...even drugs. But his mother knew nothing of this. One day alone in the attic apartment they occupied together, while the mother was out, (and she used to stay out all night drinking), he was playing at hanging himself. He had just read the life of a poet who hanged himself in a garret.

"The boy passed the heavy cord around one of the beams and stood on a box and knotted the cord around his neck. He liked to imagine the idea of dying and of being deeply regretted. He liked to picture how his mother would feel, whereas now he was faced every day with a kind of abandonment.

"Well, he tightened the rope around his neck, just playing, and then what he felt at that moment was so amazing: he felt pleasure, a pleasure that went through his body, a sensation he had never known, which started where he urinated, and then spread all over his body. It lasted only while the rope was tight around his neck.

"This discovery amazed and frightened him. He let go of the rope and went back to his books, flushed and disturbed. He could not quite believe it. Strange that where his limp little sex had been before there were great disturbances as if it were filled with a new impetus, and that was not to urinate. A kind of sap was rising and lifting it and

hardening it, just at the moment when the cord had
tightened around his neck.

"The boy told nobody about this. He wanted to
make sure it was real. He spent a restless night
thinking he had dreamt it and that the next day he
would not experience the same pleasure.

"He patiently waited until the next evening
when his mother was out again, and then he
climbed on his soap box and placed the noose
around his slender neck and pulled slightly.

"The sensation returned. When the cord was
tight something delicious and exalting happened in
the region of his sex, something never felt before
and which was a greater pleasure than that of
drinking. He enjoyed this for a few minutes and
then stopped because the blood was rushing to his
head and his neck was hurting.

"But for several nights he experienced this,
waiting always to make sure it was real, and that it
depended on the rope. He tried to make it last. He
stood there and pulled his head downward, the
rope tightening, and watched his own body in its
ecstasy of erection. His face grew congested, but the
pain around his neck he did not mind.

"The pleasure began always slowly, like wine
drinking, a warmth, then a fluid would rush to the
sex and fill it like a precious liqueur, and the
tautness was exciting and filled him with the desire,
vague and mysterious, which he could not fulfill. All

of this was a mysterious thing to him. He was afraid to tell his mother and even his comrades. He felt he had made a discovery. The pleasure was so tremendous he was almost jealous of sharing it. He felt obscurely that he would be severely scolded, more than for smoking or drinking. The tension brought about was so great that it exasperated him at times. There was something he could not discover, and that was how to release the tension of this taut joy that almost broke him when it came.

"One night with his head in the tight rope, he let his pleasure invade him slowly. It started in the middle of his body. It flowed all through him, making the body rigid, and burning, filling his little sex with something more potent than liquor, something that ached to be pushed out. That was what he felt, the desire to push it out into space. Perhaps if he tightened the rope a little more... He held his head down to watch his body. The acuteness of the pleasure forced him into a contortion which resembled the contortion of an ejaculation. He pushed his body forward, slipped off the box, and fell into space. As he fell what he had desired happened. But he was not alive to experience it."

"What a terrible story," said the Portuguese. "No wonder you can't sleep."

"There are times when one feels pleasure like this, with almost a desire to put an end to it, it is so strong."

"Would you like me to come over and we'll light the light and talk until you get over your evil impressions?"

"Yes, do come..." said the model.

The Portuguese entered her studio, looking very tall and very dark, filling the room with his vivid and potent presence. The woman's mouth could be seen in the darkness. He lit a candle, and in its flickering light she smiled at him...it was all he could do not to throw himself upon her. Her mouth was so inviting, so swollen...as if for kissing.

He sat near her bed and they talked. But as they talked she fell asleep, and the Portuguese was able to look at her. Her dark hair was all over the pillow, a dark pillow, all around her. Even in the candlelight her mouth shone red, and it was half open like a flame.

The Portuguese approached her and gave her a kiss. She awakened and put her arms around him. He kissed her again. The mouth melted under his strong lips. It was warm and soft and cushioned, as no mouth he had ever tasted.

It yielded to his kiss, opened, and the tips of two tongues met. Her breasts were so hard he felt them against his chest as he kissed her.

What he felt was that he wanted to do something to her that no other man had done—he did not want her to laugh as she had laughed for the others—he wanted to experience something new, and he did not know what it would be.

The minute she laughed she would be the woman all men could possess, and he did not want this. He continued to kiss her and think about it. Something she had not felt yet, laughed at, with pleasure. What new pleasure could he give her?

The story of the boy haunted him. He wanted to frighten her. Above all he wanted her not to laugh, as she had laughed for the other men. The way she abandoned her mouth made him hate her...the way she closed her eyes. She closed her eyes and opened her mouth as if any man, any mouth or penis could please her at the moment.

She was in a trance. Soon she would begin to laugh hoarsely and suggestively if he touched her. First he gripped her backside fiercely with his two hands and brought her up against him, and she felt his virility. It was of such strength and power that she felt it first against her hair, before it penetrated her; she gasped at the electric touch of it.

He buried his mouth deeper into hers, feeling every nook under her lips, under her tongue, feeling her tongue licking at him, flung back at his tongue each time, like a palpitation and vibration between them.

He did not caress her. He pushed himself straight inside of her, firmly, powerfully and then lay still. She had never been so well filled, every nook of her flesh filled by this strong virility, and it seemed to her that once inside of her it stretched a little more, pushed the walls of her soft flesh, installed itself leisurely, for good.

That was what she loved, the way he nestled inside of her, so completely as if to stay. She could enjoy him leisurely too. She loved this. The feel of the hard sex inside of her, not moving, nestled there, and only vibrating when she contracted to feel it more. Imperceptibly at times he withdrew, just slightly, as if to make room for the contractions which pressed him, and lured him back into the depths of her.

She did not laugh. She was strangely silent. The quietness with which he entered her, without caresses, and the quietness with which he lay inside her, as if to feel every motion and ripple of her flash around his sex. The quietness and hardness of his penis filling her completely, so that when the womb began to breathe, as it were, inhaling and exhaling there in the dark, to envelop him, encompass him and then open like a mouth and close again, she felt a quiet, long, drawn-out pleasure, which made her silent.

He was enjoying reaching into the depths of her and not moving, not giving her an active pleasure. They lay entangled, his naked body the whole length of her, and she flung back, legs apart, and eyes closed, and their mouths together.

Then the pleasure was too much for her; she wanted to move, to push against him, to feel him deeper, to cling and rub against him, but he prevented her from doing so, with such a strength of his powerful sailor muscles that she was paralyzed. Without moving inside of her, his bigness, and hardness, stirred her. She continued to lick and press and caress him with her womb, trying to engulf him more, trying to move more inside of herself since he didn't let her move her body.

Her body he kept pinned and paralyzed. Then as she contracted and moved she felt her pleasure increasing, and she was nearing her paroxysm, and out of her closed mouth there struggled to escape some guttural sound, from the depths of her belly, that would have been laughter of pleasure if he had permitted it, but he suddenly flung his two hands around her neck and whispered fiercely: "If you laugh I will strangle you!"

A strange fear came into her eyes; the sounds of pleasure died suddenly, but she could not stop the mounting, invading pleasure like some molten magical lava beginning to pour through her veins, inflaming her flesh, and he kept his hands around her throat, and she thought that her pleasure was all that mattered; she felt suddenly like the boy that she must have her ultimate pleasure for she could not control it, the violence with which it ran through her veins and sought to explode in her.

In her fear, she was immobilized, yet she continued to contract in her womb and he felt this, and it gave her pleasure to see that pleasure was getting hold of his body too, and that he might be forced to release his grip on her throat, but he did not release it—he tightened it—and she experienced a real and absolute fear then, that in his pleasure he might strangle her, for his pleasure was mixed with hatred, hatred to think she could so easily be made to feel this joy, responding to it like a perfect animal, not to him alone, but to all...to any man with a mouth to kiss, and an erect penis...

In spite of the fear, and with the fear there came a surcharged, tense joy in her, running through all her veins, tickling the soles of her feet, running up along the inside of her legs, touching off the backside and warming it, touching the tips of the breasts as if he were caressing her, nothing but this wine of desire coursing now all inside of her, and the pain of his hands on her neck could not stop it—it increased.

If she had laughed obscenely with her pleasure he would have tightened his hands, perhaps strangled her. But instead of laughing, as her pleasure was so excruciating, and as he did not move and therefore did not bring it to an end, but prolonged the excruciating suspense, a strange long whining sound came from her as if she were in pain, a deep animal whine which he loved and which then threw him with new fervor on her and loosened his hands, and then he moved, he moved in all directions, like a tourniquet, round and round, not stopping, as if he would plough her completely and absolutely, leaving no corner untouched, and she moaned, she did not laugh, she moaned in the grip of such a deep joy that she wept...

She had another admirer who was excessively timid, who in act dared nothing except follow her surreptitiously about, waiting for he did not know what. Spying on her. He had often stood at her window looking into her room, but as she put out the lights to make love, he could never catch anything but the preliminary gestures. Besides, when the Portuguese became her faithful companion, he took care to bring down the shades.

Pietro had never known a woman. In their presence he began always to stutter, to blush, and ended by taking flight.

He was twenty, also a fisherman. Vigorous, heavily tanned; blue-eyed, and with a great awkward charm in his movements.

He followed her like a detective, unknown to her. So stealthily he walked, so well he knew where to hide when she turned her head, so familiar with the whole town and surrounding roads. As she slept most of the day and was active at night she had had no time to get sunburnt. And she wanted to. But she did not want a partial one, and she began one sunny day to walk far out of town towards the beach looking for a place where she might lie in the sun.

Pietro was following her.

She wore shorts and showed beautiful legs, walking gracefully, with a slow, feline motion. She showed a firm and full backside, a waist very much indented where it should be, and breasts that stood provocatively under her shirtwaist. Her hair was free and loose, hanging all around her head and shoulders. She walked in long strides, easily, like a beautiful animal of good race. Her mouth flung open, to the wind, drinking the wind and smells of the sand dunes and pines.

Now and then the breeze wafted her odor to Pietro, and he was overwhelmed with the pungent flavor of it; his eyes fixed on her, he was in no danger of losing her scent.

She saw a place she wanted to explore. It was a rather wooded section which ran along a hilly sand dune. It was full of crevices in which she thought she might hide. Low bushes concealed her from the road where the automobiles passed.

When she stopped Pietro hid himself behind a bush which was only one yard away from her and where he could see her.

She was slowly undressing as people do in a train berth. Sitting down, so as not to be seen from the road, she was unbuttoning first of all her blouse while Pietro held his breath. Her shoulders gleaned.

Her curves were so softly rounded that she seemed to have no bones in her body. She moved every time bonelessly like a hula-hula dancer. Even sitting down she offered such undulant movements as to appear to be dancing provocatively. Her shapely shoulders appeared first, gleaming in the sun. She shook her hair away from them. Now her breasts appeared, the hard, roseate tips trembling at her movements to shake off the blouse. Like sand dunes, perfect and golden they appeared...and as she was offered some difficulties by the blouse, which pinned her arms in the back of her, in her impatience trying to shake it off she shook her breasts too, like a Hawaiian dancer, and created such disorder that it seemed she had just torn away from some secret couch of love where hands had created such a havoc with the stubbornly clinging blouse, her arms pinned over her head, and her hair and breasts mingling and getting in each other's way.

Pietro was obliged to abandon his crouching position, and to lie flat on his stomach because his muscles were trembling at the sight.

He almost wanted to beg not to be shown any more for the moment; the sight affected him so acutely he wanted to make it last, prolong the ecstasy.

For being alone, as she unveiled the various parts of her body to the sun, she had ample time to proceed to a kind of self-examination women indulge in sometimes in front of their mirror, and to do this, she lowered her head pensively and began to look at her breasts, holding them both in her hand. She was examining everything about them—the color of the skin, the nipples, the fine down around the nipples. To feel their weight and firmness, she pressed them in her hand, and correspondingly Pietro felt urged to slide his hand down into his trousers and press upon his possessions, to palpitate their weight and firmness, and he must have discovered that they corresponded exactly to the weight and firmness of her breasts, for he stopped, satisfied, and fell again on his stomach, as if the warm sand he lay on might help him to keep his turmoil in check.

Now she took off her espadrilles, and examined each painted toe, and flicked off the sand that had gathered between them. She caressed her own legs to determine their smoothness. She noticed that inside they were pale and decided to expose them to the sun.

She now proceeded to open the zipper fastener on her shorts. The zipper had marked her left side rather cruelly and to efface this she began to caress and smooth the skin down until the red marks almost disappeared.

The pleasant odor of femininity, warmed by the sun, was wafted to Pietro concealed behind the bush. He inhaled it ecstatically.

As she leaned over her breasts touched her knees. Pietro's eyes clung to them, their loveliness, their richness.

She was pulling down the shorts, rolling them down from her legs, and helping to free herself from them by lifting one leg over the other in the air, and finally she was naked.

Her skin seemed to take the sunlight and reflect it back again with more and more luminousness. She was honeyed and golden now, like some precious honey.

She arranged her clothes in a heap to serve as a cushion, and then stretched herself to the sun with the same voluptuous gesture of abandon a woman made to the approach of a man. She offered her parted legs for the sun to throw discreet rays between them, perhaps at the most vulnerable spot of all. She invited him to penetrate everywhere, in the most secret places. Pietro was envious and jealous of the permissions granted to the sun. She offered her parted legs, her round belly, her breasts, her half-open mouth, and then closed her eyes as if to permit him all the privileges.

Pietro was left with all the weight of his idol's body under his eyes, within touch of his hand, but he was too terrified to do anything but contemplate it adoringly and keep himself close to the sand to behold it and to withhold his desire, keep it from bursting. Whether it was the sun, or the warmth of her body reflecting it, or her sweet feminine odor, whatever it was Pietro had never been so drunk in all his life, nor so feverish. He feasted his eyes.

The way he was placed her legs stretched towards him, and only the most powerful timidity could restrain him and keep him from throwing himself upon her.

He pressed his sex against the sand in utter distress, wondering how he could free himself of that explosive desire, fearing its consequences. In his excitement the penis had burst through the opening of the trousers and lay buried in the sand, where it had made itself a warm nook. The sand yielded to its ecstatic pressures, like flesh, only brittle and ticklish and, at times, hurtful. But he could almost imagine that this pressure was being exerted between the legs of his adored woman.

Who knows what Pietro might have done next, for the sand contained his fervor temporarily, but when she made a movement to slightly alter her position, the sight of her undulations was driving him crazy and he might have lost his control. But a strange thing happened.

She appeared to have fallen asleep. But she wasn't. The warmth of the sun had touched her like a magical wine, and inflamed her blood too. Without any image of a man caressing her she had been responding to the burning caresses of the sun on her skin.

The sun had caressed her all over, even to the secret places between the legs. It had warmed her mouth and her nipples, and the heavy, thick lips of her sex too. In answer to its caresses somehow, her own hand moved slowly to the place between her legs where the sun seemed warmest. As if seeking its rays, as if it were another hand, she searched for its incisive caress to meet it...and found the lips it had touched into sensibility.

Warm...how warm they were. The eyes of the sun, and the hidden eyes of Pietro from behind the bush had been throwing lustful glances over them. She smoothed down the fever which agitated the lips, with cooler fingers, which had been hiding under her hair, under the shade of her dark hair. She smoothed the feverish sex mouth, as if to quiet it, to lull it.

Pietro had never seen fingers so delicate. With their brightly painted nails, the finely moulded fingers, the long, elegant outline of the hand, this beautiful hand touching the sex mouth as if it were playing on a stringed instrument—smoothing, lulling...

However, the effect was not lulling. She retained her slow lulling rhythm, but her legs made an imperceptible dance, almost. Imperceptible to all but Pietro's fascinated eyes, a slight tremor, a vibration that touched the toes and slightly curled them, swept over her.

The flower-like lightness of the fingers, and then suddenly, her other hand that had been asleep came forward too, and she opened her legs to make room for it. Both hands were required to smooth the mouth of her sex, so red and full and taut in the sun, where Pietro could see every line and nuance of it.

In the sun her pubic hair shone like a jewel, and her sex too, covered with some delicate moisture, the origin of which Pietro did not know. It was as if her fingers had called forth a hidden source of moisture, touched off the secret holder of woman's perfume. It must be this that filled the air with a feminine odor, which was turning Pietro's head. The marvellous odor; the fingers had opened a perfume bottle in the center of the woman's body.

The fingers remained quietly working, hypnotically, but the legs trembled now and then, as under a secret electric current, and now and then she raised the middle of her body as if the fingers were teasing her, as if she were about to begin her hula-hula dance... The stomach dance of the Arabian woman. Yes, she was beginning it, right there on the sand, under the burning sun, she was moving like a hula-hula dancer, while the fingers continued, as if unconcerned, to try and smooth her down.

Instead, it gave her a mad, hysterical motion of the belly and sex. She undulated and shook and jerked. Then she took her two hands between her legs as if they were a knife cutting into her and rolled herself around them, folding and doubling up her body around them, as if they were trying to do things to her which hurt her.

And to Pietro's amazement, she doubled up around her two hands and continued her dance, her hula-hula dance, ending in one motion as if she were being definitely wounded, and then falling back exhausted, panting, as if thoroughly murdered by her own caressing.

During this spectacle, without knowing why, Pietro had been compelled to imitate her movements, only having no need of a hand, merely moving around his own hard instrument of virility buried in the sand, and stirring the sand with it, and moving around it, and he too was taken with a frenzy and made a kind of dance against the sand, accelerating at the same time she did, and falling back exhausted exactly at the same time too...

As Pietro carried about his obsession with women without ever satisfying it, it was like carrying lighted dynamite, and it interfered with all his occupations. Most of his time he prowled about the beach, following the women who walked far off by themselves, hoping to assist again at the same spectacle.

But most women he met with lay dutifully in the sun, and the sun must have refrained from arousing their sensual natures, or perhaps they had no sensual nature to arouse, for they lay naked but unconcerned there on the sand, and for Pietro the real expectation was in witnessing an auto-erotic performance such as he had witnessed that first day...

Poor Pietro; his desires weighed heavily on him, and his timidity was greater than his desire. He lived in a picturesque shack, filled with fishing nets and fishing implements, a ship bed in one corner, and windows all over the Bay.

As he lived alone, a little girl eleven years old would call for his laundry and deliver it once a week. She was the child of an Italian, a girl with long, heavy hair and enormous eyes...quick, bird-like motions.

One day she came as Pietro was slipping on his trousers. For this he would sit on his bed, for he was a lazy fellow, and then begin to slip them on, and only at the last would he get up and give the final pull. He was sitting on the edge of the bed with his trousers half pulled up when the little girl knocked impetuously and without waiting for an answer, walked in with her package.

She was not flustered at all by the sight which so much resembled her father's dressing in the morning in the one room they had for the whole family. She merely stood there with her big eyes wide open and wondered where she should deposit the package.

Pietro pointed to a chair. She dropped it there swiftly and was about to turn and leave when he said to her: "Come here. I want to pay you, and besides, I have candy for you."

"You have candy?" said the little girl, approaching Pietro with shining eyes.

He pulled a paper bag out of his pocket, a bag he had been carrying about for her for two days now.

She stood one yard away from him now, with her short little dress starched and clean, above her knees, her long hair on her shoulders, and her little sweater tight around her little body.

He smiled at her with a child-like innocence, like her own smile, showing such softness that she felt as if she were facing another child.

He said, "Sit on my knees and I'll give them to you."

She approached him and sat on his knees. Her little dress was so short that her legs were bare as they settled over Pietro's equally bare legs. His trousers had fallen back to the floor, and he sat in his short white underwear, with the little girl's bare legs touching his own hairy and dark brown ones.

She was not displeased with the situation. But he was not pleased with the side-wise pose she had taken.

"No," he said, "sit facing me." She obeyed, smiling, and sat on his knees facing him.

Pietro was happy; his happiness was becoming as great as that day on the beach. The touch of the little girl's legs on his was warm and penetrating, and sent currents of pleasure all over his body.

He took a piece of candy out of the package and fed it to her. He watched her open her rosy little mouth, neat and small like the inside of a cat's mouth, the tongue so smooth and quick, and agile… He watched her close her lips over the piece of candy and then began to chew it, and with pleasure, she commenced a sort of dance over his knees, shaking herself from right to left in the joy of eating the candy.

He said, "Sit nearer. You are going to fall." So that now she sat very near to the middle of his body where the turmoil was taking place, and the edge of her frilly skirt almost touched him. Their bare legs touching and warming each other and she dancing over them accentuated his emotional state.

He fed her another candy.

He watched her voracious little mouth, too small yet for a man's kiss, he thought, but so roseate and neat and adorable. She danced again over his knees.

Pietro was growing afraid that if she moved any more an accident would happen, so he finally gave her the package and let her go.

Near the door already, she felt an excess of gratitude and she came running back to him and flung herself against him, falling with her whole weight over the part that had become so powerfully aroused, and making him gasp.

Pietro held her against himself for a moment, and then let her off, as he wanted really to press against her as he had pressed against the sand.

Then suddenly she saw the state he was in, and laughed: "You get like my papa when he kisses me in the morning."

"He kisses you in the morning—and how?" asked Pietro.

"This way." And she leaned over him and gave him her tender little girl's mouth, something more soft and delicate than he had ever touched.

Pietro kissed it, but with timidity.

"You don't kiss me as my father does," said the little girl. "Kiss me harder. He bites me."

Then Pietro permitted himself to outdistance his rival in kissing. He abandoned himself to his real desire and took the little girl's mouth in his and kissed it voraciously. She seemed pleased. She passed the back of her hand over her mouth as if to efface the traces of the strong, biting kiss and smiled again.

"And your father...he gets like this every morning?"

"Yes," said the little girl, laughing. "It comes right through his clothes."

"But what happens then?"

"He makes me kiss it too, quickly."

This Pietro could not bear. He had been containing himself long enough. Now he said, "And would you kiss mine if I asked you to?"

"Yes," she said. "You are younger than Papa, and it will be nicer."

And with her little hands, quite expertly, she took it out, charged and to the bursting point, and admired it: "It is better looking than Father's," the little girl said.

She put her little mouth to the tip only, and there on the tip of the penis she began to kiss it like a moth, now and then sucking it, so that Pietro was in a trance and fearful of whet he would do when the time came. It seemed to him that one more of those small, sucking kisses tantalizingly set upon the tip of his penis would drive him wild.

But he contained himself to enjoy the full flavour of these particular kisses. He did not want the little girl frightened; he wanted her to come back; he wanted this continued forever. It was such a teasing, the delicacy of it, the remaining at the tip, which is all that she could encompass in her small, roseate lips, and the tender, child-like way she sucked at it as if it were candy, sucking conscientiously at it until Pietro himself moved away, ready to lose his mind and fearful of harming her.

"Is that all you do to your father?" he asked, in a strained, burning voice.

"Yes," said the little girl, "that is all; after a little while he lets me go and calls for my mother. That is the way it is every morning while she makes the breakfast...and then he calls her and they lock themselves in."

So Pietro sent her away.

P ietro by now was reaching such a feverish condition that he went out in the street determined to visit the whore house. At least there his timidity might vanish.

The whore house of Provincetown was not difficult to find. The whore walked up and down the main street, and slipped her arm through that of a man walking alone, and said: "Hello."

She had the most tremendous breasts Pietro had ever seen. They came up high, under her chin, hard and round, like a tray before her, something so provocative and appetizing and violently obvious, that one could barely notice anything else. And it seemed natural when a man saw this openly pointed and offered breast that he too should respond with something pointed and forward moving in his body. It seemed the only answer possible to this display of rich and mellow and pointed sensuality.

Thus did Pietro feel every time he saw her; every time he saw her he stopped walking; he was forced to by the imperative response of his virility to this female exposure of wealth.

Her breasts were so apparent and compelling that he could think of nothing else. He wanted, in fact, to touch the breasts only.

She had often tried to lure Pietro, but aside from falling into a trance he had never answered her invitations actively. She thought he did not desire her. But she tried over and over again, just the same, and tonight more eagerly than ever because Pietro was really growing handsomer every day and particularly lately, he had such a feverish, disquieting look in his dark eyes.

This time he answered: "Where can we go? Do you want to come to my place?"

"Yes," she said, and closed her arm around his.

When she started to take off her skirt first of all, he asked her not to, only her sweater. She was left thus half-naked with her breasts spread and pointed before him. How hungry he was for them.

He wanted to slip his virility between them, and see it sliding between them. She let him; she liked the sight of this big, brown, smooth penis slipping between her swollen breasts. If it came near to her mouth she would touch it with her tongue.

But Pietro allowed her nothing but the touch of the tip of it, and when her hands grew too heavy or too experienced, he withdrew, capriciously. He wanted to be teased so lightly, and kept between the swollen breasts, like a man forbidden still the ultimate entrance.

A tiny drop appeared on the tip of his penis, like a pearl. She smiled and put her mouth to it.

Her breasts enclosed him tightly, and he pressed his hand over them.

Then a strange thing happened. He heard voices next door to his, and it was the voice of the full-mouthed friend he had watched on the beach, and she was with her Portuguese lover. Now he realized that he did not want this woman, but the other who had undressed before him and caressed herself. Suddenly his desire for the woman with the rich breasts beside him died. She was amazed and showed contempt for him.

She had not heard the sounds next door. Then she saw his desire grow powerful again. True, he looked distracted. He was trying to imagine himself embracing the other woman. He followed the progression of the sounds. He took the same position he imagined they had taken. From the sound of her voice he would tell that the Portuguese was lying with his full weight upon her, the way her voice sounded half crushed at times, and he took the same position over the whore; and then he heard the woman in the next room making the curious lament of pleasure which sounded as if she were being exquisitely tortured, and in rhythm with the voice and with his eyes closed, imagining he was taking the full-mouthed women, he pounded into the woman who lay under him.

Suddenly he heard quite clearly the woman next door saying, "No, I won't let you do that." And there was a silence.

Pietro stopped, too, withdrew from the amazed and angry whore, still erect end dripping and glistening from all the caresses.

She could not get him to continue. She determined he was quite mad, let him pay her off, and went away storming and humiliated for the first time in her successful career.

Pietro sat on the edge of his bed, wondering. What was it she had not let the Portuguese do to her? What was it he had asked of her? Such a determined sound in her voice, even anger, and it must have been serious enough for them to interrupt themselves in the middle of a full-blown séance, when she was already heaving and lamenting with pleasure.

This obsessed him. There was absolute quiet next door. If she spoke it was to refuse him, and then he evidently sulked. They must have fallen asleep, for complete silence came for the rest of the night.

The next day Pietro met her in the street. She had never noticed him, so shy and self-effacing he was in her presence. But now he looked at her boldly, taken with his curiosity to the point of forgetting all else.

Pietro spent his entire nights trying to imagine what his neighbor and the Portuguese did together, going over all the known gestures of possession and then stopping always at this mysterious request she refused to fulfill. From the sounds he could detect when it was that the Portuguese was lying on top of the woman. When he fell with his great weight over her the bed had a certain heavy way of creaking.

When it was she who sat astride over him, the difference in weight was obvious to the attentive ears of Pietro. He could tell too, when they lay spoon fashion, as then the bed swung from side to side and occasionally bumped the wall. From his voice too, he could tell when the Portuguese was using only his tongue, for then her moans were small and short and light, or his fingers.

Then the strange scene repeated itself. In the absolute darkness Pietro heard distinctly her voice: "No, that I won't do."

He could visualize the Portuguese crouching over her, stopping perhaps in the middle of their bout, his penis all glistening from its sojourn inside her excited womb and he whispering this request in her ears, which she would not consent to.

"Please," he begged. "Please. Just once. I will never ask you again."

Then Pietro could not bear the suspense and he slid out of his bed and crouched all the way to their window. There was a powerful moonlight which drenched their bed.

And Pietro could see them clearly, she bathed in the light and naked, and he indeed crouching over her and begging.

Then suddenly they disentangled their limbs, all entangled together, and left the bed. The Portuguese stretched himself on the floor, absolutely relaxed. She still resisted, but at the same time the softness of his voice lulled her, enchanted her, his pleading.

She stood over him, legs akimbo, and with her back to his face. She remained rigid and said: "I don't think I can do it, even if I wanted to pleasure you."

"Try," begged the Portuguese, "I will help you. Just relax."

With his two hands on her legs, he slightly pushed her to obey him, and forced her downward, to crouch. As she bent down her backside came right near to his face. With his two hands, he forced her to crouch this way over his face and when she was placed just where he wanted her, he began to caress her clitoris with his two hands, a strange little caress, palpitating it, as if to draw something from it.

"Do it," he pleaded, "do it, my darling. Feel my finger there? Let it flow, let it come, do it, for love of me."

She remained in position, but she could not obey him. He continued to caress her. Then suddenly he uttered a cry of joy. She had relaxed and was urinating, and it fell over his face and he was in ecstasy, his penis erect, and for fear she should rise and stop he held her backside to his face with his two hands.

And Pietro watching, remained transfixed, baffled, for he could not understand why he suddenly wished to be in the Portuguese's place.

I n the fourth studio lived a beautiful young man, slender and stylized, who practiced every day in the open air his trapeze work.

For this he wore the tightest white tights imaginable, and as he was extremely sun-burnt, he looked like a slender Indian, with his glistening black hair and dark skin.

As he studied his movements, Pietro re-marked how tightly he kept his backside pressed together; it was almost a vice. He walked pressing it together almost as if he feared being attacked from behind. It was so obvious that it irritated Pietro who liked relaxed and opulent figures. The way he compressed his backside as he moved. It was irritating. It almost made Pietro want to force it open. But he contented himself with watching the boy exercise every morning over his im-provised bars.

In the evening he exposed some of his auda-cious trapeze acts at one of the night clubs.

Pietro and he struck up a sort of friendship. The trapezist liked to have an audience, and Pietro faithfully attended his acts and applauded them when they reached their perfection.

Then one day the trapezist, while resting, told Pietro his story:

He was a star in a New York circus. Every night he performed wearing the most beautiful satin tights and silk shirt. His figure was very much admired, prized even, among the perverts. He attracted both men and women.

One night he received a vast quantity of flowers from an admirer. He was accustomed to this; he merely glanced at the card which accompanied the flowers. The name was unknown to him, but a comrade who was there whistled, "Oh, one of the richest men, an English aristocrat. You're a lucky dog. He'll make your fortune. He'll take you around the world in his yacht."

The Lord was discreet and noble. He came into the box and sat down, made beautiful conversation.

He had handsome hair, grey...he was attractive in every respect. His blue eyes were innocent, his smile delightful and humorous. He entertained them all as he watched them dress, undress, change for the performance. The glance he gave to the trapezist was that of a connoisseur. He complimented him on his perfect figure, his cat-like strength, which did not appear in any over-development of muscles, his agility. He was almost like a dancer on his trapeze, possessed of supreme audacity and elegance.

His new admirer rather pleased him and flattered him. He thought he might now enjoy a bit of a vacation with him. He was pretty tired of his continuous performance.

The elderly Lord was charming, still so slender and beautifully dressed. He sat in the box several nights watching the young trapezist dressing, looking over his silk shirts, his satin tights, his slippers, his colored stockings, and brilliant shirts. Then one evening he said: "Will you come and have dinner with me?"

The trapezist expected this, was flattered and accepted. He dressed himself more carefully, but the Lord asked especially to keep his trapeze tights on, underneath the city suit. They were made of white satin, tightly fitting, showing the contours of the backside of the young man, and certainly all of the outline of his sexual possessions.

The Lord watched him with a smile of admiration as he dressed. The trapezist thought it would be easy enough to yield to him. Such a charming man. So civilized and cultured and witty.

They went off together in the Lord's powerful car.

They rode out of New York City, and after half an hour stopped before a sumptuous house. An exquisite dinner awaited them, served silently and smoothly in a huge dining room.

Then they smoked and drank the finest liqueurs, and then when they went up to the Lord's bedroom, the beauty and warmth, the charm and luxury completely enveloped the trapezist who had never seen anything like this, and who was ready to yield to the Lord's desire at any moment.

The Lord stood near him and watched him undress. First the coat, the tie, the shirt. He admired his magnificent arms again, and from under the arms came an odor which the Lord loved, the odor of young perspiration. He inhaled this and continued to watch the young man undress; to take down the pants he balanced himself perfectly and leaned over. Now he stood in his white satin tights, so slender and perfectly made, while the Lord admired him, but without touching him. The Lord's breath was accelerating, however, and the trapezist was flattered by his excitement.

Then, with all the insidiousness of a strip-teaser, he set about to take off his white satin tights, prolonging the moment as he felt he was causing the Lord such an intense pleasure. At first he pulled the front and exposed his genitals which were as beautiful as his body, and then very slowly and gradually he exposed the neatest, most tender backside, like a young girl's. The skin was delicate and satiny. He turned his back to the Lord, knowing this was the part of a man's body such men prized above all, to give him the full sight of this upturned backside, to arouse him fully.

All of a sudden he felt something like a violent slap on one side of the exposed backside.

Instinctively his hand rushed to the beaten spot, and he felt a warm rush of blood. He withdrew his hand and looked at it, dazed.

The Lord spoke quietly, "Don't be alarmed. It is all over."

He pressed a button. "I have a doctor and nurse here. They will fix you all up. I will give you plenty of money, all you need. It is nothing. Have no fear. That is all I wanted from you."

He had slashed a long opening in the most tender part of the backside with a razor.

The door opened, the doctor and nurse appeared, they tended to him, and the next day he was sent away with a goodly sum.

But something remained in the trapezist beside the scar. The habit of closing his backside tightly, as if in fear of being attacked.

I n between the artists who lived in the wharf studios there lived perfectly bourgeois families who came from Boston on their vacation, with their children, and who objected furiously to the nature of the conversations and noises which came from their neighbors.

Whole families who reported the quarrels and obscenities that they heard, whole families who reported to the police that they had seen a woman naked on the beach, a few miles off from the place where they had been sitting.

These people revealed remarkable sensitivity of ear and eye, almost an over-development. It was as if they had actually been straining to catch these undercurrents of amoral lives which surrounded them. But slowly the amoral element was winning out and it was the families who were obliged to look for houses further removed from the pernicious influence of the artists.

What facilities for acquaintances, at the beach, on the road, in the dunes, under the showers, everywhere, in fact. And in the evening about seven or eight night clubs shed their red lights through the town, and spilled their music out in the street for everyone to hear and be tempted. Smoky night clubs, dug sometimes under street levels, sometime on the wharf again, over the rush of bay waters, smoky and densely populated, ideal for straying hands and knee brushings, and foot signals under the tables, and for soldered dances, and secret appointments. The population mixed with the summer visitors, the lovely Portuguese girls, the models, the painters.

If a dancer came to the town he or she was immediately used for modeling for the painting classes. Whoever had a bit of beauty or interest or character served the painters for subject, and one could watch them at work on the beach.

But there came to Provincetown a Viennese mime dancer "from Europe." At first she stood at the cafés and street corners chatting with her friends, and one could hear her vivid descriptions of the concentration camps where she had been. She was telling hair-raising stories of her sojourn in one of them. She had been picked up around Mont-parnasse, and, being Jewish, was incarcerated, finally released after, she said, agreeing to sleep with the entire division of German soldiers.

Now she was exactly made for this vivid role, being extremely voluptuous in her shape, and walking with a most accentuating swing of the hips. It was clear even from her walk why she had been selected as capable of satisfying a division of German soldiers. But she insisted that it had cost her days at the hospital afterwards, before she was finally fit to sail for America, and once here, able to resume her dancing.

This story had a peculiar effect on her audience. Somehow, one could never see her without imagining her lying down and, with her two legs in the air, serving her sentence, as it were, under the passage of the German soldiers. And she added: "They were timed by the Captain. Not allowed more than five minutes to do it in."

One listened, and the eyes were drawn to her legs. Now there was one peculiarity about her legs. That is, way beyond the place where one is accustomed to expect hair, she bore the traces of recently shaved-off hair, a dark area far below the rim of her bathing suit. The eyes were always fixed there during her story. It was a wonderful story to make men concentrate on her sexual parts and cease to see her face, which was not particularly beautiful. This excess of hair gave her a strange animal quality. One expected savagery from her. One wondered if she had submitted, without biting or clawing, to her fate in the concentration camp.

Men had a peculiar feeling about women whom they know to have been frequently sexually used. It relieves them of their timidity. This explains the success of the old actresses in Paris, from the Music Hall, well-worn women, through which most of the Parisian theater-going crowd had paid homage of the most intimate kind.

This feeling pervaded the Viennese dancer... It was a kind of invitation. One was certain of not being rebuked. She was practically assuring one of a welcome. If she could welcome so many German soldiers, surely she would welcome any amount of assaults from friendlier sources. It was truly a form of encouragement she dealt each time she told her story.

Such were the feelings she aroused in Pietro who was seeking to rid himself of the obsessional fixation upon the full-mouthed girl. He began to haunt the steps of the Viennese dancer.

However, he made no headway. The dancer grouped him with her other friends, took him to the beach, to the night club, danced under his eyes, but never permitted him to approach her further.

Pietro was baffled.

He knew himself to be handsome, handsomer than the rest of her friends.

One night at the night club, now dense with smoke, voices, music, where she stood making her breasts dance, not moving from the waist down but only the bust and shoulders, which gave to her breasts a curious savage rhythm, Pietro caught her eyes on him and responded with all the desire he felt, and he saw her eyes waver for the first time.

Hot and perspiring, she came to his table, asking for a drink, which he gave her. Then she said: "I'm tired, Pietro, you can take me home."

She was still in her dancer's costume, which consisted of a short, tight dress, the dress of Kiki of Montparnasse, the escaped school girl dress with long black stockings.

They walked together up the long, winding street and then turned into one of the dark wharves.

Pietro said: "Sit with me on the sand for a little while."

They descended the steps of the wharf and found themselves lying on the sand, next to the heavy beams overhead, and the little waves lapping at their feet.

She lay on her back with one leg curved and her arms behind her head.

"What are you thinking about?" asked Pietro, hoping she would talk again about the concentration camp.

And indeed she did. She was always remembering it. She was easily led into talking about it. They had taken her into the Captain's tent. Naked. Absolutely naked. Then the Captain had stood outside and let the soldiers in, one by one.

All of them had been deprived of sexual intercourse for a long time. The duties had been severe and burdensome. They were all excited by the idea, before even seeing her. When they came into the tent they were already exalted, excited, with all their blood in their genitals ready to explode.

At first it was not bad. The first ones were so ready for it that they did not mangle her too much. A few short strokes, and they were ready, and they did it quickly, being rushed by the Captain at the entrance. And then, as she filled with the semen, it made it easy for the passage. She was oozing liquid, all wet with it.

But these were the young ones who came easily and did not belabour her intensely; when the older ones came, she was already sore from so many possessions, and they took longer and needed more pushing and pressing...it was hurting her. Her moans of complaint aroused them to even greater thrusts, aroused their savagery.

They held her legs back and fell upon her without a single caress or word, like animals, intent only on emptying themselves.

When the Captain came she was bleeding and weeping. Then they took her to a hospital.

Here ended her story, but Pietro felt that she did not tell all.

"What were the consequences?" He asked. "Did you hate men after this?"

The question amazed her. No one had asked it before.

She was silent and then she said, "No, I did not hate men, but I could no longer feel anything; I was cold. Ordinary love-making seemed tame and dull to me. This coldness lasted until I met a Catalonian in New York. But I can't tell you...this I can't tell you."

"Tell me," said Pietro, "I am a friend."

"This Catalonian had a special collection of objects from the Chinese quarter in Barcelona. He had them all exposed in a glass cabinet in his bedroom. He showed them to me. We returned from a ball, and I was beautifully dressed...he had taken me back for a last glass of champagne. For the first time since that incident at the concentration camp, I was interested, stirred, in fact. I stood in front of the cabinet and looked at those implements, and he saw that I was interested. He was an attractive man, smooth, smiling, an elegant and wealthy demon, he was. Slender and refined, and with grey hair on his temple. A perfect aristocrat. There was a story about him and a trapezist, but it was not proved.

"What a smile he had, the true smooth satanic smile of a man who had seen everything. His hands were the longest-fingered hands I have ever seen. Pliant and white and beautifully cared for with heavy rings, which accentuated their fragility and aristocracy. His teeth were small and rather pointed, sharp like a wolf's teeth. His skin was pale and transparent like a woman's.

"When he saw my interest, then he took a little key and unlocked the cabinet, let me look at each implement. He picked one up, which was an arti-ficial tongue with two strings tied to it so that it could be tied around the head over the mouth.

"This was a heavy rubber tongue with rubber spikes all over it. When the Catalonian put this on, he looked like a monster, no longer like a man. He looked terrifying, and at the same time, to me, infinitely seductive. His eyes had changed expres-sion. He now had a look which matched the tongue, a look of lust and cruelty.

"I was stirred. He saw it. He pushed me gently but unwaveringly toward his big canopied bed. He pushed me so that I fell upon the bed. He pulled up my dress and let me feel the tongue through my underwear at first, just so I would know its spiked feeling before it touched my flesh.

"Well, the feeling I had then, that I was going to be caressed by a superhuman man, unlike other men—that resembled the fear and terror I had when I lay naked exposed to the soldiers in the camp. A feeling of the inhuman that might give me a sensation never known before.

"I felt him tugging at my underwear, dealing knowingly with the unhooking of it, the sliding of the panties down over my knees. I raised my head. This spiked-tongued monster was now burrowing between my legs. Each time he moved I felt the rubber spikes bristling against the softest part of my skin, the skin in the inside of the legs, around the sex.

"Such a strange sensation. I had never experienced this feeling before, that it was some strange animal touching me and not a man. What excitement, to feel this strange touch of rubber spikes. And he did not touch the sex right away. He lingered.

"It felt at times rough like a dog's tongue. Have you ever felt a dog's tongue on your hand? Or a cat's? Rough and scraping over the skin. He stopped to place a pillow under my head so that I could raise my head and watch him. He wanted to be looked at. Perhaps he wanted to enjoy my terror.

"I looked at him with dilated eyes, waiting for the moment when he would try to caress me intimately with the false tongue, fearing the pain and yet curious of the feeling it might give me.

"He had caressed me all around the clitoris, and was now approaching it. There he began to lick me, and to arouse me by his persistent caresses. So much so that I relaxed and the honey began to flow.

"When he saw this he tried to place the tongue between the mouth of the vulva and caress me. It scraped against me, stirred me, hurt me, and yet somehow excited me so that I wanted it further in.

"He pushed it in. It was hard pushing, the spiked parts met with resistance; and I closed my eyes. It seemed to me that I was being raped all over again, only this time I was enjoying it.

"Then I felt a strange thing, when my eyes closed the spiked tongue belaboured me, and at the same time I felt his sharp tongue in my flesh, all over the tender parts, biting incisively and rousing me to a kind of fury and frenzy. I moaned and he laughed then. Now he handled the tongue sharply, disregarding any gentleness, and he inserted and pulled it out again, like a penis.

"Then he left me writhing there and said: 'Don't move. I am bringing you something even more wonderful.' He returned and stood at my side near my face so that I could see that over his own erect penis he had slipped a huge rubber one, considerably lengthened and equally hard, with rubber spikes on it too.

"This huge instrument he held to my face until he saw that I was growing afraid. Now I was afraid. It was bigger than anything of the sort I had ever seen and I was afraid to have it inside of me.

"Suddenly I remembered the craziest passage from the Bible.

"I remembered how I had read this when I was a young girl, that I was excited by it without quite knowing why, and it was about some women who were not satisfied with men and who sought the enormous penises of donkeys, who had dealings with donkeys.

"Now it was before me, and I began to tremble, and at the same time I was in a state of great excitement with a fever and curiosity and tension which were stronger than my fear.

"He placed it at the entrance and waited. It would never go in. I am rather small, if anything, but as he placed it there I remembered all those soldiers who had penetrated me, and some of them had such huge members, and I remembered it felt as if they were pushing my womb open to make room for themselves.

"And now the Catalonian stood at the entrance and was pushing equally without paying any attention to my last-minute resistance, for it was so powerful and big and painful that I wanted to draw away from it, and he did not let me. He pushed on regardless, and all through the pain I felt the most exquisite joy. Finally I let him, and once he had pushed it in he couldn't move it because it was so immense. I felt so strange...then after a while he withdrew and let me lie there panting and yet satisfied, but so aroused that one more touch would set me off...

"He returned with the strangest penis of all, a rubber penis all ridged around like a tower of Pisa, a circular staircase of ridges from the tip of it to the bottom, and this he inserted; it clutched at my flesh...once inside he turned it over, and its ridges seemed to touch parts of me that no man had ever touched and to arouse me in a way no penis had aroused me, the way it scraped and pushed my flesh, every part of it.

"I was about to come, but he would not let me...he immediately withdrew when he saw me coming near to my pleasure. He wanted to prolong it. Now he brought one shaped like the figure of Napoleon, with the three-cornered hat and everything painted on. As he pushed it in, the corners of the hat, made of rubber, yielded, but once inside it took its natural shape again, and I felt them in my womb, the three points like the points of a star, lodged against my flesh. When the Catalonian began to withdraw it, I felt it caught inside and sharply pointed against my flesh, hurting me and at the same time touching me off where the penis never went, places which responded electrically to the pointed sharp edges of Napoleon's hat.

"The Catalonian was laughing. I began to laugh hysterically, shaking my body. Then he began to bite me. As he buried his teeth into my flesh I shivered with pleasure. He bit me over and over again and he made me come this way, sinking his teeth into my flesh at the very edge of the sex."

Pietro was aghast. Such a woman he could not hope to satisfy. He remained silent. She began to laugh in the dark. She understood what had happened to him...

BOOK TWO

MARCEL

Marcel came, his blue eyes full of surprise and wonder, full of reflections like the river. Hungry eyes avid, naked. Over the innocent, absorbing glance fell savage eyebrows, wild like a Bushman's. The wildness was again attenuated by the luminous brow and the silkiness of the hair. The skin was fragile too, the nose and mouth vulnerable, transparent, but again the peasant hands, like the eyebrows, asserted his strength. As he stood there he was constantly in mutation between fierceness and assertiveness, and sudden eclipses of his whole being. Constantly oscillating even in the same moment, between his appetite which opened his thick sensual mouth and some pale secret flame of unreality sapping his strength. A sudden confusion that flowed from the ever-surprised eyes, from the golden halo over his fine hair, and the wildness of the eyebrows and brutality of the hands.

In his talk it was the madness which predominated, his madness of analysis. Everything which befell him, everything which fell into his hands, every hour of the day was constantly ripped apart, commented upon. He could not kiss, possess, desire, enjoy, without immediately commenting, relating, describing. He planned his moves beforehand with the help of astrology; he met with the marvellous often; he had a gift for encountering, for inspiring it, for evoking it. But no sooner had the marvellous fallen to him than he grasped it with his peasant hands, grasped it with the violence of a man who was not sure of having seen it, lived it, and who longed to make it real.

I liked him just before he talked. I liked his pregnable self, sensitive and porous, just before he talked when he seemed a very soft animal, or a very sensual one, just before he talked when his malady was not perceptible. He seemed then without wounds, walking about with a heavy bag full of discoveries, notes, programs, new books, new talismans, new perfumes, photographs. He seemed then to be floating on like the house boat, without moorings. He wandered, tramped, explored, visited the insane, cast horoscopes, gathered esoteric knowledge, collected plants, stones.

"There is a perfection in everything that cannot be used," he said. "I see it in fragments of cut marble; I see it in worn pieces of wood. There is a perfection in a woman's body that can never be achieved in intercourse, that can never be possessed, known completely.

"I am always left with a hunger, with a hunger for the insolent perfection of a woman's belly, for the white wickedness of her hips, of her ass. I am never through fucking, I am never through gathering everything in the world, collecting carved bone from the Arctics, collecting cloths, glass, sea-weeds, because there is nothing that I can ever possess.

The essence is always beyond me, unseizable, tantalizing."

He wore the flowing tie of the Bohemians of a hundred years ago...the cap of an Apache, the coat of a horse-racing man, or the striped trousers of the French bourgeois. Or he were a black coat like a monk, the bow tie of the cheap actor of the provinces, or the scarf wrapped around the throat of the "pimp," a scarf of yellow, of bull's blood red. Or he wore another suit given to him by a business man, with the tie flaunted by the Parisian gangster or the hat worn on Sunday by the father of eleven children. Another day he appeared in the black shirt of the conspirator, another, in a checkered shirt like a peasant from Bourgogne, another day in a work-man's suit of blue corduroy with the wide baggy trousers. At times he let his beard grow and he looked like Christ. At another time he shaved himself and often he 1ooked like a Hungarian violinist out of an ambulant fair. I never knew in what disguise he was coming to see me. If he had an identity, it was the identity of changing, of being anything, the Moroccan, the Laplander. It was the identity of the actor for whom there was a continual drama. His arrival was an entrance upon a stage. Every movement had the tension of a movement made within the drama.

His occupations were equally changeable and multiple. One moment he sat reading the meaning of handwriting at a café table. He could tell a stranger unexpectedly some intimate detail about his character. "When you go home the first thing you do is take your shoes off, put the shoe horns inside them and put them away in your closet." At another time he might be lecturing at the Sorbonne on his tour of Lapland with slides. The slides would appear upside down during the lecture and he would lose the thread of his description. The people would grow restless, and he would come out pale and haggard from the effort of communicating to others the marvels of a trip made marvellous by his own imagination. He was always outside. He liked to write his lectures and articles at a café table. Preferably where there was music. His favorite pastime was to be able to sit at a café table on the boulevards and watch the whores. He would make up stories about them, how they would fuck, how they would look in furs, in robes of damask lying on black velvet, in Tibetan castles nude with heavy bracelets of copper. He loved the illusion of luxury. He was born the son of peasants. Luxury transported him. He knew nothing about the world of rich people and he had woven extraordinary fancies about them. He gave this world a coating of brilliance and magic it never actually had. He endowed it with supernatural marvels. If I talked to him about its hardness, its boredom, its gift for marring every pleasure by lacking the true capacity for enjoyment, so that every marvellous scene created by luxury was always eaten as by worms by the attitude, the character of the people who possessed it, I could never convince him. For to him there was always the feeling that the richness was a sort of Arabian magic. He would sit for hours in luxurious cafés enjoying with half-closed eyes the velvety sounds, the music, the brilliancy of the women, the elegance of the men.

Marcel in the streets, cafés, movies, in the Bohemian quarters, in the night club quarter, walking, smelling, seeking, observing. He could never see or hear enough. He was always hungry for motion, people, crowds, change, incidents, adventures. He spent nothing on food so that he could buy things, the fetish, a Chinese gong, incense, some object for his apartment.

There is always lightening in his eyes. I feel his intensity. He is saying, "Alan is the man like a diamond. He is pure and no one can disintegrate him. You are the myth woman; you have the beauty of the women of the myths."

It was raining on the floor of the house boat. Marcel and I sat on the floor looking through the contents of his bag. The river was like a mirror. At five o'clock Paris always has a current of eroticism, it is in the air. Is it because it is the hour when the lovers meet? The five to seven, of all French novels. Never at night it would seem, for all the women are

married and free only at "tea time," the great alibi...
At five I always felt shivers of sensuality, shared
with the sensual Paris. As soon as the lights fell, it
seemed to me that every woman I saw was running
to meet her lover, and that every man was in a
hurry to meet his mistress.

When he leaves me, Marcel kisses me on the
cheek. His beard touches me like a caress. This kiss
on the cheek which is meant to be a brother's is
charged with intensity.

Marcel said: "You have never come to see my
apartment."

"No, but I had a dream about it," I said. "It was
high up, a high place. And it was crowded with
marvellous objects."

"That is absolutely true, that's amazing," said
Marcel.

"I will come someday."

Marcel lay on the bed looking at the painted
ceiling. He felt the cover of the bed with his hands.
He looked out the window at the river.

"I like to come here, to the barge," he said. "It
lulls me. The river is like a drug. What I suffer from
seems unreal when I come here."

"What do you suffer from?"

"Oh," Marcel cried. "So many things. I feel I am
a failure. I cannot accomplish anything. People
always ask me what is my occupation. I don't know
what to say."

"Your occupation is to walk through all of them in a state of transparence, to live only in extracting the meaning and the essence, and within the frame of none to walk out and beyond all occupations and experiences. You are the poet and the adventurer."

"How true," said Marcel. "You have understood that. Why don't other people? They always say, 'You have not written your book on Lapland. You have not given your conference on the reading of the handwriting.'"

I talked to disentangle the knots of his life. We talked on, but he was dead. A great trouble came between us. A brother, a brother, I felt, but there is too much warmth and when I felt the delicate bristle of the Christ-like beard, I was stirred. He left the house boat as if I had hypnotized him. I danced in the room. Unless you love him, I said to myself, do not radiate this warmth. Close yourself. But I have no doors to close on this ecstasy. Mandra, Mandra, you said he was a brother. Do not play with his love.

I wanted to play with Marcel. I wanted his nearness.

We had dinner together. I suggested we go dancing. We went to the Bal Negre. Immediately Marcel was paralyzed. He was afraid of dancing. He was afraid to touch me. I tried to lure him into the dance, but Marcel would not dance. He was awkward. He was afraid. He was far from me, congealed with fear. When he first held me in his arms he was trembling, and I was enjoying the havoc I caused. He was nervous. I had been tabooed. I was the wife of Alan whom he loved like a brother, I was from another world than the one in which he had been born, I was an artist, I was a personality. He said, "I have never known a woman like you."

I felt a joy at being near to him. I felt a joy in the tall slenderness of his body. I wanted him to dance, but he was rigid with the taboo. I said, "Are you sad? Do you want to leave?"

"I'm not sad, but I'm blocked. My whole past seems to stop me, I can't let go. This music is so savage. I feel as if I could inhale but not exhale. I'm just constrained, unnatural."

"It is my fault, Marcel. I felt so much that you had my rhythm that I wanted to dance with you. I felt dancing was natural, necessary."

After these words, suddenly the tension in him loosened. He held me very close, and I felt the currents passing between us, waves of intoxication—but still intermittently broken by fear. I did not ask him to dance anymore. I danced with a negro.

When we left then in the cool night, Marcel was talking about the knots, the fears, the paralysis in him. I felt the miracle had not happened. I will free him by a miracle, not by words, not directly, not with words I used for the sick ones. What he suffers

I know. I suffered it once. But I know the free Marcel. I want Marcel free. But, Mandra, you bitch, if you do it, if you do it with love, you will kill him. You're drunk, but not with love. He will be drunk with love. He has a need. He has not known anyone like you. You know that. You are ten years older.

I feel an immense wave of tenderness. I feel like enfolding him, protecting him. That is more like it, Mandra. Be a sister. But what a passionate sister I am. I cannot be trusted.

I am luring him away from the Sorbonne, from the Psychological group, from Montparnasse into a pure poetry. He looks like Christ but his mouth is sensual, thick, almost like a negro's. His ears are small and delicate. His whole body is full of the contrast between the animal and the spiritual.

He wrote me the first letter to reach me in the little letter box, saying, "Your house boat will be Noah's Ark in a troubled, tragic time. It will sail away with everything that is worth saving. It will be Noah's Ark in the inundations of politics and hatreds, floating alone, saving what must be saved from this and of the world."

But when he comes to the house boat and sees Hans there, when he saw Fiametta hovering around me, following me like a shadow, when he saw Gustavo arriving at midnight and staying on after he left, Marcel got jealous. I saw his blue eyes grow dark. When he kissed me goodnight he stared at

Gustavo with anger. He said, "Come out with me for a moment, Mandra."

I left the house boat and walked with him along the dark Quays. Once we were alone, he leaned over and kissed me passionately, furiously, his full mouth drinking mine. I offered him my mouth again.

"When will you come to see me?"

"Tomorrow, Marcel, tomorrow I will come to see you."

When I arrived at his place he had dressed himself in his Lapland costume to surprise me. It was like a Russian dress and he wore a fur hat. He wore long felt boots which were black and reached almost to his hips.

His room was like a traveller's den, full of objects from all over the world. The walls were covered with red rugs; the bed was covered with animal furs. The place was close, intimate, voluptuous like the rooms of an opium dream. The furs on the bed, the cloth walls, the deep red, the objects like the fetishes of an African priest—everything had an erotic violence.

I wanted to lie naked on the furs, to be taken there lying on this animal smell, caressed by the fur.

I stood in the red room of this desire and Marcel undressed me. He held my naked waist in his hands. He explored my body with his hands, eagerly, desirously; he felt the strong fullness of the hips.

"For the first time a real woman." he said. "So many have come here, but for the first time there is a real woman, someone whom I can worship."

As I lay on the bed it seemed to me that the fur, the smell of the fur and the bestiality of Marcel were all mixed, combined. Jealousy had goaded him and broken his timidity. He was like an animal, hungry for every sensation, for every way of knowing me.

He kissed me eagerly; he bit my lips with excitement. He lay in the animal furs, kissing my breasts, feeling my legs, my sex, my buttocks. Then in the half-light he moved up over me, shoving his penis in my mouth. I felt my teeth catching on it as he pushed it in and out, I felt them scraping against it, but he liked it; he watched me, he was watching and caressing me, his hands all over my body, his fingers everywhere seeking to know me completely, to hold me. I threw my legs up over his shoulders, high, so that he could plunge into me and see it at the same time. He wanted to know everything. He wanted to see how the penis went in and came out glistening and firm, big. I held myself up on my two fists so as to offer my sex more and more to his thrusts. Then he turned me over and lay over me like a dog, pushing his penis in from behind, with his hands cupping my breasts, caressing the clitoris, with his arms around my body, caressing and pushing at the same time. He was untiring. He would not come. I was waiting to have the orgasm with him, but he postponed and postponed it. He wanted to linger, to feel my body forever, to be endlessly exalted. I was growing tired. I cried out, "Come now, Marcel, come now." He began then to push violently, moving with me into the wild rising peak of orgasm, and then I cried out, and he came almost at the same time. We fell back among the furs, released.

We lay in half darkness, surrounded by strange forms, by magical forms of a sort of sex-sleighs, boots, spoons from Russia, crystals, sea shells. There were Chinese erotic pictures on the walls. But everything, even a piece of lava from Krakatoa, even the bottle of sand from the Dead Sea, everything had a quality of erotic suggestion, the object which was the symbol of the unattainable body of desire.

"You have the right rhythm for me," Marcel said. "Women are usually too quick for me. I get into a panic about it. They take their pleasure and then I am afraid to go on. They do not give me time to feel them, to know them, to reach them, and then they come and I go at crazy after they leave thinking about their nakedness and how I have not had my pleasure. But you are slow. You are like me. You are slow too."

"No, I have learned to hold it until I feel that I am in rhythm; one learns that. To hold it back until the right moment."

"That is wonderful, Mandra. With you I felt I could take my time and not be afraid. With you I felt that I satisfy every desire. It is the first time that I have come on time with a woman."

"But Marcel," I cried, "You have known so many women. How can that be possible?"

"It is true I have had a great many women, so many that I cannot remember their names at times. But you know how it is, it is usually some young girl from the university, some woman I have met sitting at a café. There is always a strangeness, an awkwardness with a new woman. I know nothing of her likings or dislikings. It makes me a little shy. So I am always worrying about their getting their pleasure and so very often I do not get mine. In one night you have not got time to find out about the temperament of a woman, you do not have time to feel her out, to know her rhythms, her reactions. It is all fumbling in the dark, and the pleasure is not so profound."

As he talked I thought about Hans, about Gustavo; when you love somebody, sometimes a year or two later you discover greater and deeper sensual harmonies. The knowledge between the bodies grows and we come into greater ecstasies, acquiring the understanding and accord with the loved one's responses, desires. The desire which is satisfied with the stranger is the desire of the skin. It is only the lovers who can know this, for slowly the deeper, the more profound desires are awakened between them. They enter the limitless levels of sexual ecstasies which can exist between those whose knowledge of each other increases.

"I never know the woman I bring home"—Marcel went on holding me in his arms and talking in the twilight of his room which he had built to create desire. "I am always uneasy. I do not know what to do. I know that if I do not please her she will never return. I can never be free to really love, to discover a woman because I have always the thought like a barrier that she will not come back, that she will not like my love-making. I have a desperation because I know that I can never discover a woman in one night."

"Sexual joy," I said, "is like a dance between two people. When it is free, unpremeditated, then something magical takes place. Ecstasy only comes when there is no timidity, when there is no longer a question about how the other person feels. Ecstasy comes only when we fulfill our desire. Sexual knowledge must be blind. It is a way of knowing with the body itself. When you worry if the woman will come back, when you wonder how to satisfy her—you have choked off all passion. When you are afraid of your desire, thinking about its effect, its meaning, then sex becomes a gesture: a questioning that you can never satisfy a woman, you can never come to know her desire. It is when you abandon yourself freely and without questioning to the movements of your own body, it is when you enter blindly the passionate rush of your own desire that you can come to know your lover."

Marcel took a piece of cedar from Lebanon in his hands, caressing it. "I wish I could have one woman for myself," he said. "Every day I would want to touch her, I would come to know some new part of her. Every part of me would come to know her. I want to live with a woman until I am really satisfied, until I am complete. I don't want to go on this way, always half satisfied, and feeling that I have only half possessed a woman. I want to reach the very bottom of love, to know a woman through and through, all that she likes, and to be relaxed in her presence, knowing she will be there as long as I want her to be."

"There are things we can know in sex only after a long time," I said. "That is what I have had with my lovers, the ones I kept for a long time. A passion such as I never had from one night with anyone."

"I wish you were free to love me, Mandra. I know there are Alan, Hans and Gustavo now; I know you are not free."

"We will find you a woman, Marcel," I laughed.

"There was a girl who almost seemed to be the woman for me," he said, "the one I finally took to Lapland. I met her on a bus in the summer at Chauxcrutte. She was wearing a flimsy, light dress that showed her figure. She was standing at the platform of the bus, breathing the air as if it were a great living pleasure in itself. What a body she had, Mandra. Every curve of it showing, revealed by the dress. I wanted to touch her breasts under the cloth. When she sat down I sat opposite her. Her skirt was very short and she was tall so that when she sat down I could see right between her legs to where the stockings stopped. She had a free sort of life about her. When she moved her legs she seemed to be opening them up, to be inviting me to touch her. There was a willingness about every movement of her body; there was a willingness about her dress, about the way she sat. Finally I spoke hesitatingly. Would she have an aperitif with me? She consented and we sat together in a little café. She would move her legs up against mine under the table. When I felt up her leg, feeling the pubic hair under her pants, she would go on talking, looking at me with her eyes shining, youthful, joyous.

"Then she came home with me. She stood by my window. I said to her in a low voice: 'Lift up your dress. I want to see it.'

"She took off her dress and stood in the afternoon light naked. She moved toward me, putting her arms around my neck, kissing me, moving her naked body against me.

"She liked everything. She loved the fur, too, as you did. She had a wonderful body. It was completely sun-burnt. She used to lie at the bottom of a boat and get naked and let the sun burn her all over, even between the legs. She confessed that the sun made her passionate, it excited her. Whenever she took a sun bath, she would lie masturbating lingeringly, slowly. I asked her to do it for me. She said she would not do it with her fingers but with a banana, that the banana once it was peeled was so much like a penis, that it would get warm and wet like a penis. I made her do it in front of me. Mandra, it was something you can't imagine, the way she behaved. The convulsions, the sight of the banana lying between her legs, the way she teased herself with it, touching herself at first only with the tip of it, and then suddenly thrusting it in.

"I was always excited by her. But every time she came sooner than I did, and then I could not go on, even though she said all the time, 'Go on, go on, I like it. Make me come again, make me come!' But I could not do it. I took her to Lapland with me. Do you know what I did? I bought myself a fake penis, one that fills with warm water.

"I caressed her all over, lying over her and driving her crazy. It was as if she had two men making love to her. While she sucked my cock I would drive the other penis into her. She gripped my legs in her ecstasy; her nails cut into the flesh. I did it all together, touching her everywhere with it, and then this way I was sure that once she had come, I would not mind my own penis dying down. As soon as she came, though, I had not come; my penis would always be afraid then, it would lose its madness, it would question. Now I was no longer embarrassed. I would go on pushing the false penis into her, I would go on with the false penis, and she would get excited again. I found that I got excited too, that once the fear of not being able to go on once she had come was gone, then the impotence was gone and I would get hard again. Finally I was able to come and I discovered that she liked it the second time more than the first; the first was only a little prelude. She liked the second orgasm better; her whole body would seem to rise to it. That is the nearest I ever came to a real harmony with a woman. But do you know? It never could be done without the fake penis. She took a liking to it, as she had for the banana. She liked it more than the real penis, she said. Can you believe this? She wanted me to make love to her with just the false penis sometimes. She began to masturbate with the false penis. She didn't seem to need me. She would wear herself out in the afternoon lying in the sun with her eyes closed, biting her lips, twisting her legs about the penis that was filled with warm water. She seemed so alive to me in the beginning. Even her masturbating with the banana was exciting to me; it seemed to quicken the life in me. But now when I came to her she was jaded. She was not satisfied with my body. She was no longer interested. I was impotent again and finally we separated and I returned to Paris."

As I dressed we stood by the fireplace in Marcel's room talking. When I was all dressed, Marcel slipped his hand under my skirt and began caressing me again. We were suddenly drunk, blind again with desire. I stood there with my eyes closed and feeling his hand, moving upon it. He gripped my ass again with his hard peasant grip, and I thought we were going to roll down on the bed again, but instead be said, "Lift up your dress."

I pushed up my dress, leaning against the wall moving my body against his. He put his head between my legs, seizing my buttocks in his hands, touching my sex, sucking and licking until I was wet again. Then he took his penis out and took me there against the wall. His penis, hard and erect like a drill, pushing, pushing, thrusting up into me while I was all wet and dissolved in his passion.

Gustavo was telling about the time in Argentina when he took ether. He took so much that he fell on the floor with convulsions, and when he came back to consciousness be found himself covered with his own sperm. He had a friend who was an acrobat in a circus. This friend had red hair, freckles, a long lanky body, and he could never find a woman who wanted him. So he took to the habit of rolling himself up into a ball and taking his own penis in his mouth and sucking it in front of anyone who wanted to watch him. He only did it in front of people who were shocked by the sight of this animal red head of hair buried between its own legs like some mythological animal.

Gustavo had another friend who liked to exhibit himself. He never had intercourse with women. What he liked was to find some dark street and when a woman passed by he opened his coat and showed himself naked. This gave him the most intense pleasure. When he went to the Bohemian Montparnasse parties, in the middle of one he would ask, "May I show myself?" And immediately begin to take his pants off. Sometimes he was chased away, sometimes tolerated, and then walked about exposing himself, his penis, showing it to the women. Merely to be looked at gave him an erection. And now and then it brought him to an orgasm, especially if the women looked interested and continued to watch him with any interest.

His greatest pleasure came when he moved to an apartment house overlooking a girls' school. He watched them all day playing in the yard. He would stand by his window and watch the bare legs of the girls as they ran and played games. He would take his penis out and watch the little girls running and playing about. His penis would get erect, and then sometimes when he could not control himself he would stand by the window naked and show himself. As soon as a little girl saw him he fell into a trance of pleasure and he would come while she looked at him, not understanding sometimes why this man was shaking so at the window.

With Gustavo himself I enjoyed it more than with Marcel because he had no timidities, no fears, no nervousness. He falls into a dream; we hypnotize each other with caresses.

I caress his neck, the nape of his neck and pass my fingers through his black hair. I caress his belly, his legs, his hips. When I touch his back from neck to buttocks his body begins to shiver with pleasure. He likes caresses like a woman. His sex stirs. I don't touch his sex until it begins to leap. Then when I touch it he gasps with pleasure. I take it all with my hand, hold it firmly and press it up and down. Or else I touch the tip of it with my tongue, and then he moves it in and out of my mouth. Sometimes he comes in my mouth and I swallow the sperm. Sometimes it is he who begins the caresses. My moisture comes easily; his fingers are so warm and knowing. Sometimes I am so excited that I feel the orgasm at the mere touch of his finger. When he feels me throbbing and palpitating it excites him. He does not wait for the orgasm to finish; he pushes his penis in as if to feel the last contractions of it. His penis fills me completely—it is made just for me, so that he can slide in easily. I close my inner lips around his penis and suck him inwardly. Sometimes the penis is larger than others and charged with electricity, it seems, and it is as if we were electrically soldered, magnetized; then the pleasure is immense, protracted. The orgasm never ends.

Women very often pursue him, but he is like a woman, he needs to believe himself in love. He can get excited by a beautiful woman, but actually when he is lying in bed with her if he doesn't feel some kind of love he is impotent.

It is strange how the character of a person is reflected in the sexual act. If one is nervous, timid, uneasy, fearful, the sexual act is the same. If one is relaxed and easy going the sexual act is relaxed and enjoyable. Hans' penis never softens so he takes his time; with the certainty about it, he installs himself inside his pleasure as he installs himself inside of the present moment, to enjoy, calmly, completely, to the last drop. Marcel is more nervous, uneasy, restless. I feel even when his penis is hard that he is anxious to show his power and that he is hurrying, driven by the fear that his strength will not last.

Last night after reading some of Hans' writing, his sensual themes, I raised my arms over my head. I felt my satin pants slipping a little at the waist; I felt my belly so vividly; I felt my belly and sex so alive. In the dark Hans and I threw ourselves into a prolonged orgy. I felt that I was taking all the women he had taken, everything that his fingers had touched, all the tongues, all the sexes he had smelled, every word he had uttered about sex, all this I took inside me, like a big orgy of remembered scenes, a whole world of orgasms and fevers, and I devoured everything as Hans and I were devouring each other in a dark banquet of teeth into flesh, and flesh soldered together by currents of ever-returning desires.

Marcel and I talk together lying on his couch. In the semi-darkness of the room he was talking about a friend of his who complained of not having a capacity for adventures. "When it is an adventure I feel nothing; I tried many times, but I was impotent. Yet I would like it, I would like to be free of love. Often I have fits of eroticism and the woman I love at the moment may not be in the same mood or she may be sick or away from Paris. I would like an adventure then. I dream of it. I have tried it so many times, but I cannot feel. I can only feel when I am in love and then it is marvellous—such violent erotic nights I have had. But why can't I enjoy one night, a woman I like for a moment, anyone I see who appeals to me?

"I like to follow women in the street, their perfume. I follow them for a whole day sometimes. At crowded hours I like to stand on the platform of the busses and be pushed against young girls. And they like it too, the little shop girls. They let themselves be squeezed and they enjoy it. Another time I sat next to a whore in the bus. I was reading a paper; I put down a part of it on my knees and suddenly I felt a hand feeling around my penis. I did not move. It was the most marvellous sensation. I kept looking out of the window and the whore kept her hand on my penis until I had a tremendous erection. Then she said, 'Will you come with me and treat me to an aperitif?' I went with her; we sat at a café. She was a nice whore from the south of France, with brilliant eyes and a fresh, lively body. We went to her room. She worked me over, you cannot imagine; she did everything to get me roused but I couldn't. I tried to think of pictures I had seen in the penny movies, to think of a woman I had desired at one time or another..."

Marcel told him about the rubber penis and how he used it to excite and satisfy the women in cases like these. Marcel was talking about erotic fantasies he had and how difficult it was to satisfy them. He always wanted a woman to wear a lot of petticoats and he would lie underneath and look. He remembers that is what he did with his first nurse and pretending to play he had looked up her skirts. This first stirring of the erotic feeling had remained with him.

So I said, "But I'll do it. Let us do all the things we ever wanted to do or imagined done to us, if you want to. We have the whole night. There are so many objects here that we can use. You have costumes too. I'll dress up for you."

"Oh, will you?" said Marcel. "I'll do anything you want, anything you ask me to do."

"First get the costumes. You have peasant skirts there that I can wear. We will begin with your fantasies. We won't stop until we have realized them all. Now let me dress..."

I went to the other room, put on various skirts he had brought from Greece and Spain, one on top of another. Marcel was lying on the floor. I came into the room. He was flushed with pleasure when he saw me. I sat on the edge of his bed.

"Now stand up," said Marcel.

I stood up. He lay on the floor and he looked up between my legs, under the skirts; he spread them a little with his hands. I stood still with my legs rather spread as if for a dance. Marcel looking at me excited me, so that very slowly I began to dance as I have seen the Arab women do, right over Marcel's face, slowly shaking my hips so that he could see the sex moving between the skirts. I danced and moved and turned and he kept looking and panting with pleasure—then he could not contain himself; he pulled me down right over his face and began biting and kissing me. I stopped him after a while. "Don't make me come, keep it."

Then I left him and returned naked, wearing his black felt boots. Then Marcel wanted me to be cruel.

"Please be cruel," he begged. All naked, in the tall black felt boots, I began to order him to do humiliating things.

I said, "Go out and bring me a handsome man. I want him to take me in front of you."

"That I won't do," said Marcel.

"I order you to; you said you would do anything I asked you."

Marcel got up and went downstairs. He came back about half an hour later with a neighbor of his, a very handsome Russian. He had told the Russian what it was we were doing. The Russian looked at me and smiled. I did not need to arouse him; when he walked toward me he was already roused by the black boots and the nakedness. Marcel did not want this to happen. I made him witness. I not only gave myself to the Russian but I whispered to him, "Make it last, please make it last."

Marcel was suffering. I was enjoying the Russian, who was big and powerful and could hold it for a long time. Marcel was watching us but his penis was out of his pants and it was erect. When I felt the orgasm coming in unison with the Russian, Marcel wanted to put his penis in my mouth but I would not let him. I said, "You must keep it for later, I have other things to ask you, I won't let you come!" The Russian was taking his pleasure; after the orgasm he stayed inside and wanted more, but I moved away.

The Russian said, "I wish you would let me watch..."

Marcel objected. We let him go. He thanked me very ironically and feverishly. He would have liked to stay with us.

Marcel fell at my feet. "That was cruel, Mandra; you I know that I love you. That was very cruel..."

"But it made you passionate, didn't it; it made you passionate."

"Yes, but it hurt me too. I would not have done that to you."

"I did not ask you to be cruel to me, did I? When people are cruel to me it makes me cold, but you asked for it, and it excited you."

"What do you want now, Mandra?"

"I like to be made love to while looking out of the window, while people are looking at us. I want to feel the secrecy of it. I want you to stand next to me and take me from behind, and I want nobody to be able to see what we are doing... I like the secrecy of it."

I stood by the window...people could see into the room from other houses...and Marcel came up from behind and took me from behind as I stood there. I did not show one sign of excitement, but I was enjoying him; he was panting and could scarcely control himself. He was all ready to come, and as we stood there I kept saying, "Quietly, Marcel, do it quietly so that nobody will notice."

People were looking at us as we stood there; they thought we were just standing there looking at the street and we were enjoying the orgasm as couples do sometimes under doorways and bridgeways at night pretending to be standing very still, to be embracing quietly…

We were tired. We closed the window. We rested for a little while…we began to talk in the dark as if we were dreaming and remembering.

"A few hours ago, Marcel, I entered the subway at the rush hour, which happens rarely. I was pushed by the waves of people, jammed, and stood there. Suddenly I remembered a subway adventure Alraune had told me about, when she was convinced that Hans had taken advantage of the crowdedness to caress a woman and at the very same moment I felt a hand very lightly touch my dress, as if by accident. My coat was open, my dress light, and this hand was brushing lightly just the tip of the sex. I did not move away. The man beside me was so tall that I did not see his face. I am not sure it was he, and I did not want to see the man. I did not want to know who it was.

"The hand caressed the dress; then very lightly it increased its pressure, feeling for the sex. I made a very slight movement to raise the sex toward the fingers. The finger became firmer, following the shape of the lips deftly, lightly. I felt a wave of pleasure. As a lurch of the subway pushed us together, I pressed against the whole hand and he made a bolder gesture, gripping the lips of the sex. How I was frenzied with pleasure. I felt the orgasm approaching. I rubbed against the finger, and imperceptibly the finger seemed to feel what I felt and continued its caress until I came. The orgasm shook my body. The subway stopped and a river of people pushed out. The man disappeared."

She was much more like fire than light. Her eyes were an ardent, violet color. Her hair was dyed blond but it shed a copper shadow around her. Her skin was copper-toned too...firm and not transparent at all. Her body filled her dresses tightly, richly. She did not wear a corset, but her body had the shape of the women who did. Arched so as to throw the breasts forward and the buttocks high.

The man stood looking at her, the long finely-featured face smiling, the elegant gestures poised so delicately, making a ritual out of the cigarette lighting, and he said, "This time I came just to see you."

Mathilde's heart beat so swiftly that she felt as if this were the moment she had expected for years. She almost stood on her toes to hear the rest of his words. She felt as if she were the luminous woman sitting back in the dark box receiving the unusual flowers. But what the polished grey-haired writer said with his decadent, aristocratic voice was: "As soon as I saw you I was stiff in my pants."

The crudity of the words was like an insult. She reddened and struck at him.

This scene was repeated several times. Mathilde found that when she appeared men were usually speechless, deprived of all their romantic court-ships. Such words as these fell from them each time at the sight of her. Her effect was so direct that all they could express was their physical disturbance...

Instead of accepting this as a tribute she resented it.

Now she was in the cabin of the smooth Spaniard, Dalvedo. Dalvedo was peeling some cactus figs for her, and talking... Mathilde was regaining confidence. She sat on the arm of the chair in her red velvet evening dress. But the peeling of the figs was interrupted. Dalvedo rose and said: "You have the most seductive little mole on your chin." She thought he would try to kiss her. But he didn't. He unbuttoned himself quickly and took his penis out with the gesture of an apache to a woman of the streets. "Kneel," he said.

And Mathilde struck out like a woman of the streets, and moved toward the door.

"Don't go," he begged, "you drive me crazy. Look at the state you put me in. I was like this all evening when I danced with you. You can't leave me now."

He came upon her and tried to embrace her. As she struggled to elude him he came all over her dress. She had to cover herself with her evening cape to regain her cabin.

D avid is a young painter. When I met him at the M's house our intensity flashed danger signals at each other across the room. His face was young, luminous. His hair shone, his eyes were electric, his gestures quick, passionate. I did not think of him, because of his youth.

But the next day he sent me a telegram, "May I come and draw your picture?"

I said, "No." I had to be at the M's house for a lecture. I said, "You can come if you want to." He was disappointed not to see me alone, so he refused. But I felt that he would come. When I got to the M's he was the first to greet me. He was shy; he could not talk well, but he followed me about, just looking at me and smiling.

The next day I let him come. He sat at the other end of the studio and tried to draw me while I was writing. I felt the tension in him. I like so much that moment of tension before the explosion of desire, this leaning over a precipice. I noticed he wore a ring which was too tight for his finger, which contracted it. I asked him to take it off. He did. Then he said,

"That represents exactly the way you influence me. I feel I can breathe and expand in your presence."

Now I am back in America.

The illuminated skyscrapers shine like Christmas trees. We were invited to stay with rich friends at the Plaza. The luxury lulls me, but I lie in a soft bed sick with ennui. Like the flowers in a hot-house. My feet rest on soft carpets. New York gives me a fever, the great Babylonian city. Byzance. All gold and white, glitter and sumptuosity.

I see Lilith. I no longer love her. There are those who dance and those who twist themselves into knots. I like those who flow and dance.

I will see Mary again. Perhaps this time I will not be timid. When she came to St. Tropez one day and we met casually at the café at the Port, she invited me to come to her room in the evening.

I left Gustavo and Marcel and went to see her at eleven o'clock. I was wearing my flounced Spanish cretonne dress and a flower in my hair and I was all sunburnt and bronzed and feeling beautiful.

I was stirred by my visit to her. I could have stayed with her. Gustavo had to return that night to the place where he stayed quite far away.

I was free.

When Mary said, "Come in," I was stirred. But when I came in she was lying on her bed cold creaming her face, her legs, and her back because she had a sun-burn from lying on the beach. She was rubbing cream onto her neck, throat...she was covered with cream.

This discouraged me. I sat on the front of her bed and we talked. I lost my desire to kiss her. She was running away from her husband. She had only married him to be protected. She never loved men, but women, but her husband did not protect her.

She had told him, at the beginning of her marriage, all sorts of stories about herself that she should not have told him, how she had been a dancer on Broadway and when things did not go very well, she got money for sleeping with men, how she even went to a house and earned money there, how while prostituting herself she met a man who fell in love with her, who rented an apartment for her and kept her for a few years, etc.

The husband never recovered from these stories. It awakened his jealousy and doubts until their life had become intolerable.

The next day she sailed back...and I was left with regrets for not kissing her. Now I would see her again and I might not be so timid.

In New York I unfold my wings of vanity and coquetry.

Mary is as lovely as ever and very much moved by me. She is all curves, softness, her eyes are wide and liquid, her mouth full, her cheeks luminous, her blond hair heavy and sensual. She is slow, passive, lethargic. We went to the movies together. In the dark she took my hand. Hers was soft—soft like milk, warm, clinging.

She is being analyzed and has discovered what I sensed long ago, that at thirty-four she has never known the real orgasm, even after a sexual life which requires an expert accountant to keep track of... I am discovering her presences. She is always smiling, gay, and underneath she feels unreal, far off, removed from any experiences. She is acting as if she were asleep. She is trying to awaken by falling into bed with whomever invites her.

Mary says, "It is very hard to talk about sex...I am so ashamed." She was not ashamed of doing anything at all, but she could not talk about it. She can talk to me. We sit for hours in perfumed places where there is music. She likes places where the actors go.

There is a current of attraction between us, purely physical. We are always on the verge of getting into bed together. One night I thought of her with real desire. Why it does not happen I do not know. She is never free in the evenings. She will not let me meet her husband. She is afraid I will seduce him.

She fascinates me because sensuality breathes out of her, pours from her. At eight years she was already having an affair with an older cousin, a Lesbian affair.

I am waiting for her to be cured of her frigidity. We both share the love of finery and perfume and luxury. She is so lazy, languid, purely a plant really, with her full body, full mouth. I never saw any woman so yielding about bed invitations. She simply and naturally falls into bed when she has no feeling about it. She says that she always expects the man to come who will finally arouse her. She has to live in a sexual atmosphere even when she feels nothing. It is her climate. Her favorite expression is, "At that time I was sleeping around with everybody."

If we speak of Paris and of people we knew there she always says, "I don't know him. I didn't sleep with him." Or, "Oh yes, he was wonderful in bed."

I never heard of her resisting once. This coupled with frigidity. She deceives everybody, including herself. Men think she is in a state of near orgasm continuously. She looks so wet and open. But it is not true and this conceals a closedness. The actress in her acts cheerfully and calm, and inside she is going to pieces, drinking and sleeping with drugs only.

She always comes to me eating candy like a school girl. She looks about twenty. Her coat is open; her hat is in her hand. Her hair is loose. She falls on my bed and knocks off her shoes. She looks at her legs, "They are too thick, they are like Renoir legs, I was told once in Paris."

"But I love them," I say, "I love them."

"Do you like my new stockings?" She raises her skirt to show me.

She orders a whiskey. Then she decides that she will take a bath. She borrows my kimono. I know that she is trying to tempt me. She comes out of the bathroom still humid, leaving the kimono open. Her legs are always held a little apart. She looks so much as if she were near to having an orgasm, that one cannot help feeling; only one little caress will drive her wild. And it is tempting. As she sits on the edge of my bed to put on her stockings, I cannot withhold any longer. I kneel in front of her and put my hand on her hair between her legs. I stroke it gently, gently, and I say, "The little silver fox, the little silver fox. So soft and beautiful. Oh, Mary, I can't believe that you do not feel anything down there, inside."

She seems so much to be on the verge of it...the way her flesh looks, open like a flower, the way her legs are spread. Only one little caress, one feels, and she will surely have the orgasm. Her eyes are so wet, her mouth is so wet, her mouth is so inviting, the lips of her sex must be the same. She parts her legs and lets me look at it. I touch it gently, and in between the lips to see if they are moist. At the tip of the lips is the tiny little mount of the clitoris where she does feel, but I want her to feel the bigger orgasm.

I kiss the clitoris which is still humid from the bath, the hair which is still humid like sea weed. The sex tastes like a sea shell, a wonderful, fresh salty sea shell. Oh, Mary, Mary! My fingers work more quickly; she falls back on the bed, offering her whole sex more open to me, open and moist. She feels like a camellia down there, like rose petals, like velvet, silk, satin. It is rosy and new, as if no one had ever touched it. It is like the sex of a young girl...

She has fallen back and her legs hang down the side of the bed, loose and heavy, inert...her sex is open; I can bite into it, kiss it, insert my tongue. She does not move. The little clitoris stiffens like the nipples of a breast. My head between her two legs is caught in the most delicious languor of silky, salty flesh...a languor.

My hands travel upward to her heavy breasts, caress them. She begins to moan a little. Her own hands travel downward and join mine now in caressing her own sex. At the mouth of her sex, below the clitoris, she likes to be touched. She touches the place with me. It is there I would like to push in a penis and move until I make her scream with pleasure. I want to make her scream with pleasure... I put my tongue there at the opening and I push it in as far as it will go. I take her ass between my two hands, like a big fruit, and push it toward my mouth, and while my tongue is playing there into the mouth of her sex, my fingers press into the flesh of her ass; my hands travel around its firm-ness, into the curve of them, into the curve between the two round firm parts, and my forefinger somehow feels the little mouth of the anus and pushes it gently.

Suddenly Mary gave a start. As if I had touched off an electric spark. She moved to enclose this finger. I inserted it further, continuing to move my tongue inside of her sex...and moving the finger in her ass. And suddenly Mary began to undulate, to moan, to undulate only from the waist down, only the ass and sex moving, back and forth.

When she moved backwards she felt my finger; when she moved upward she met my tongue flicking inside of her; every move she made she felt this tongue and finger quickening until she gave a long final spasm and began to moan like a pigeon... and with my finger I felt the palpitation of pleasure, the little heartbeat of pleasure going once, twice, thrice...the little gong inside of the woman beating ecstatically.

She fell panting over me... "Mandra, Mandra, what have you done to me, what have you done to me?" Her breasts fell over my face, her kisses over my mouth all wet with her moisture; she drank the salty moisture from my mouth, she kissed me, her breasts fell over my face as she held me saying, "Oh Mandra, what have you done to me, what have you done, it was marvellous..."

I was invited one night to the house of a young society couple, the H's. Their apartment is like a boat because it is near the East River and the barges pass while we talk, the river is alive. Myriam is a flawless beauty, a delight to look at her, very big—a Viking girl, full-breasted, with rich magnetic hair, a rich voice that lures you to her magnetically. A wonderful nonchalance. He is small and of the race of the imps, not a man but a faun, some lyrical animal so quick and humorous. He loves my writing and he thinks I am beautiful. He treats me like an "objet d'art." The black butler opens the door. George exclaims over me, my Goyescas hood and red flower in my hair and pushes me into the salon to display me. Myriam was sitting cross-legged on a purple satin divan. She, the natural beauty, and I, the artificial one, who needs a setting and warmth to bloom successfully. That night in the warmth of their admiration I bloomed too. Her beauty warmed me.

The apartment is full of objects I would individually find ugly—silver candelabras, tables carrying at each end a nook for trailing flowers, enormous mulberry satin puffs and rococo objects seen in aristocratic French homes, English homes, things collected with a feeling of vast superiority to the owners, collected to be laughed at in the superior, nonchalant way as if saying, "I can do ridiculous things, I am above them, I can make fun of everything created by man and fashion, I am above them."

Ornate, varied, gathered here with the same light, snobbish playfulness, not taken seriously, "amusing," full of chicness and which an ordinary person could make impossible, but here they were like some Dadaist impertinence with an aristocratic boldness that made beautiful the collector's impudence, which only aristocrats can give to a home.

Everything was touched with that graceful impudence. I could sense through the objects that fabulous life in Rome and Florence, Myriam's frequent appearances in *Vogue* wearing Chanel dresses, the pompousness of their families, their efforts to be elegantly bohemian, their frontiers overlapping into surrealism, and that obsessional word which is the key to society and aristocratic living, "amusing." Everything was said in order that it be "amusing." I could sense all sorts of refinements, of laisser-aller, of audacities.

Myriam called me into her bedroom to show me a new bathing suit design she had bought in Paris. For this she undressed herself completely, and then took the long piece of material and began rolling it around herself like the primitive draping of the Balinese.

Her beauty was going to my head. She undraped the bathing suit, walked naked around her room, and then she said, "I wish I looked like you. You are so exquisite and dainty. I am so big."

"But that's just why I like you, Myriam."

"Oh, your perfume, Mandra."

All naked she pushed her face into my shoulder, under my hair and smelled my perfume.

I placed my hand on her shoulder.

"You're the most beautiful woman I've ever seen, Myriam."

George was calling out to us, "When are you going to finish talking about clothes in there? We're bored."

Myriam said, "We're coming." And she got dressed quickly in slacks. When she came out George said, "And now you're dressed to stay at home, and I wanted to take you to hear the String man. A man who sings the most marvellous songs about a string and finally hangs himself on it."

Myriam said, "Oh, all right. I'll get dressed." And she went into the bathroom.

I stayed with George in the salon, and the other two men with us. Myriam called me, "Mandra, come in here and talk to me."

I thought by this time she would be half-dressed, but no, she was standing all naked in the bathroom, powdering and fixing her face.

She was opulent like a burlesque queen, her hair falling long over her shoulders. As she stood on her toes to paint her eyelashes more carefully I was again affected by her body. I came up behind her and watched her. I felt a little timid. She wasn't as inviting as Mary was; she was, in fact, like the women at the beach, sexless, or at the Turkish bath, who think nothing of their nakedness. I tried a light kiss on her shoulder. She smiled at me. She said, "I wish George were not so irritable. I would have liked to try the bathing suit on you. I would love to see you wearing it." She returned my kiss but lightly. On the mouth, taking care not to disturb the lipstick outline. I did not know what to do next. I wanted to take hold of her. I stayed near to her.

Then George came into the room without knocking or warning, came into the bathroom and said, "What, Myriam, how can you walk around like this? You mustn't mind, Mandra. It is a habit with her. She is possessed with the need to go around without clothes. Get dressed, Myriam."

Myriam went into her room and slipped on a dress but wore nothing under the dress, then a fox cape, and she said, "I'm ready."

In the car she slipped her hand over mine. Then she drew my hand under the fur, into a pocket of the dress, and I found myself touching her sex. We drove on in the dark.

Myriam said she wanted to drive through the Park first. She wanted air. George wanted to go to the night club, but we drove through the Park, I with my hand on Myriam's sex, touching it, caressing it, fondling it and feeling my own excitement gaining so I could hardly talk.

Myriam talked, wittily, lightly, continuously; I felt mischievous and said to myself, "You won't be able to go on talking in a little while." But she did, all the time that I was caressing her in the dark, beneath the satin and fur. I could feel her moving upward to the finger touch, opening her legs a little so I could fit my whole hand between her legs, and then I felt her growing tense under my fingers, stretching herself as if before the climax, and she moved quicker and I knew she was taking her pleasure, and her pleasure was contagious. I felt the orgasm without even being touched.

I felt so wet that I was afraid it would show through my dress. And it must have shown through her dress. We both kept our coats on as we went into the night club.

Myriam's eyes were brilliant, deep. There were lines under her eyes. George left us for a while and we went into the ladies' room. This time Myriam kissed my mouth fully without regard for the consequences. We kissed, arranged ourselves and returned to the table...

LIFE IN PROVINCETOWN

One long main street running along the Bay outline.
Portugese fishermen sitting in circles like the Italians and chatting. Behind the houses on the main street are wharves which project out on the water at various lengths. On these wharves are the huts, shacks, which the fishermen once used to store their nets, tools, and the boats to be repaired. It is here that the artists live. The roofs are peaked and beamed. Everything is made of rough wood like the inside of some old ship. At high tide the water runs under the wharves, at low tide it exposes a long stretch of sand.

The walls are thin. One can hear everything. Oftenthe shades are not down, and one can see everything.

There are no guardians, no one to say: stop the noise, or to see at what time one comes home. No superintendents, house owners. Just the lonely wharves, in darkness at night, the sound of the water, and little crooked shacky studious occupied by a variety of people.

The town is full of soldiers, sailors, and beautiful Portugese girls......and summer visitors in shorts.

There is one movie, one bar where women are not admitted and several night clubs.

In one studio there lived one of the artist's models, whose mouth was so big, so full, so prominent, that one could see nothing else. When she looked at one, one could notice only the mouth, like the mouth of a negress. She rouged too heavily, and then powdered her face white, so that the mouth stood out even more and was able to eclipse the rest of the face and even the body.

Facsimile of page from copy no. 1